Reunited With My Billionaire

Alix Vaughn

Contents

Chapter 1

Callie

I 'm not going to miss this shower. The pressure isn't strong enough and the water never gets as hot as I'd like. I also won't miss sleeping on the lumpy old couch.

I run the loofa over my body, thinking about what's in store for me on my first day at my new job.

Thump, thump, thump. A knock at the door. "Callie! How much longer?"

"Two minutes!" I shout back.

I hear Sasha grunt in annoyance. I owe her big time for letting me crash with her for the past two weeks. With my new job as a live-in nurse, I'll be staying with my patient, so I had no need to renew my lease. Thankfully, Sasha offered me her couch. Unfortunately for both of us, she lives in a tiny studio and we are constantly in each other's way.

"Seriously, Cal, I'm going to be late for rotation!"

Sasha and I met as freshmen at NYU. She was studying to be a doctor, me a nurse. We became a dynamic duo.

Even dynamic duos can get on each other's nerves.

"I'm almost done! Relax!" I shout back. It's not my fault she can't wake up to her alarm.

I nabbed this new job after doing grunt work at the hospital for six years. Now, instead of tending to patients all over a hospital, I'm only going to have one. And, from what I understand, he has quite the bank account.

I don't know who he is, but I've signed a hefty NDA that makes it clear I must be discreet over the three months I'll spend with him.

I finish up in the shower, wrap my hair in a towel, and start to dry off. But I'm distracted by the tattoo on the inside of my left arm. I've had it for almost ten years now and to this day it still surprises me sometimes.

Happily. For the most part.

The memory behind it isn't so happy, but the message is.

I haven't truly looked at the small bouquet of daisies on my forearm in some time. Inked in sketchy black, reminiscent of the field of wildflowers near my childhood home.

Sometimes it's just a tattoo.

Other times, the thing comes to life.

And I'm right back in that moment.

—◦O◦—

Ten years earlier...

The old porch swing creaks beneath me, rocking back and forth. It's a cool August night.

I'm waiting for him, just like I have every night for the past few weeks. We meet here when the moon is out, and the sky is so dark you can see every star.

Tomorrow, he's leaving.

So tonight, I'm planning to give him everything.

I hear some movement from the wild, unkempt field next to the house. That's when I see him: muscles bathed in moonlight, looking as towering as a scarecrow in the tall grass. When he's closer, I can make out his features. Sharp jaw covered in a layer of scruff, strong brow, deep brown eyes, dark brown hair cropped tight. Everything about him should make me fear him.

But I don't. Not for a second.

Liam. Handsome, respectful, funny. My summer love.

Also, my brother's best friend. It's why we've kept our connection hidden all summer. My brother didn't bring his oil rig buddy home for a month to fall in love with his sister. I know if Nate even got a whiff of it, Liam and I would be six feet under. He's always been so overprotective.

Liam climbs the rickety front steps toward me. I try not to look eager, but it's hard when every nerve in my body is vibrating with the hope he'll touch me.

"Hey." Mmm… his voice is smooth as butter.

"Hi."

"Got these for you."

I look at the bunch of wild daises in his hand. Our fingers brush as I take them from him, and my body melts.

"They're beautiful. Thank you."

"Was nothing. Just picked them in the field."

I smile. "I love them."

Tonight is the night. I can feel it. It's the night we take it to the next level. Nate and Liam are leaving tomorrow to go back to the rig. It's now or never.

And I just know. Tonight, I'm going to lose my virginity to Liam.

"Can I sit?" he asks, nodding toward the spot next to me.

For Liam's size, his voice isn't as deep as you'd expect. When he does decide to speak, his voice is silvery, like every word is carefully chosen, meant to land in my ears like leaves falling from a tree.

The amount of poetry I've come up with for this man is embarrassing, but I can't help it.

"Of course," I reply.

Liam sits, the swing groaning beneath us. I hold the flowers in my lap tenderly. There's enough space between us for another person in case Nate or one of my parents would come out and see us. I want nothing more than to wriggle up next to him, but I'll be good as long as I can.

"What time are you heading out tomorrow?" I ask, caressing the petals of one of the flowers.

"Early. Gotta catch a bus into the city at six."

"That is early," I remark.

"Callie..."

I lift my gaze to him. There's sadness in his tired eyes. I don't blame him. I'm feeling it too. "Yes?"

Liam doesn't reply, but his eyebrows clinch together with concern.

"What is it?" I slide closer to him and put my hand on his arm.

"Ah, damn, this is hard."

I giggle and rub his arm. "Doesn't have to be. Just say what's on your mind."

Liam glances back at the house and then sighs, eyes fluttering shut.

"Hey..." I lean in toward him and kiss his cheek. "Tell me what's on your mind."

Liam turns his face toward mine like he's about to kiss me but shakes his head instead. "I'm sorry."

"What for?"

He delicately removes my hand from his arm and puts it in my lap. "This was really fun, Callie. But we have to say goodbye."

I'm not totally following. Not yet. There's a way I've imagined us saying goodbye, quietly in my bed with our bodies wrapped around each other, making sure the mattress doesn't creak beneath us. "I know we do."

"Yeah, but like, we have to *now*."

I blink.

"You know, it just wasn't ever gonna last between us." Liam swallows. "I hope you don't feel I've led you on or anything, but..."

I feel my heart start to crack, but hope is still beaming from within me. He's just confused. He's scared. That's okay. I can fix that.

"We knew this would end at some point," he says with an apologetic smile.

"We still have tonight, Liam." I bend my body toward him, press my chest against his arm. I know that he wants me. All I have to do is show him I want him. "We can still –"

Liam draws away violently. "No. We can't." He's firm and his amber eyes flicker with fire.

I can't help the wound that is forming in my heart from projecting outward.

"I'm sorry, I don't want to hurt you. But this all was a mistake from the beginning."

A *mistake*? It wasn't a mistake. Not at all.

"You know, we just never should have –"

"Is this because of Nate?" I interrupt him. I can feel heat staining my cheeks pink.

"Not exactly."

"Did he say something to you?"

"No, but I shouldn't be getting involved with his little sister. Especially when..." Liam grips the edge of the swing and looks off into the dense night. "You're so young, Callie."

I clutch the flowers to my chest. "So?"

"So...you're eighteen. You're going to go to school and experience life for the first time. You're not gonna get involved with a guy so much older than you who works on an oil rig, you know?"

"Well, why not?"

Liam laughs. "Lots of reasons."

"Why are you laughing at me? I'm not a kid."

"Yeah, you are, Callie. That's not a bad thing." He leans forward. His legs are so long that his feet can touch the ground while he's on the swing. He folds his hands between his knees. "I'm sorry I got you confused."

I don't have the strength to respond, but in my head, I have a torrent of things I'd love to shout at him. Confused? How could I be confused when *he* was the one who kissed *me*! It happened just days after he came home and met me. My body burned with desire for him after we when we ran into each other... literally. How could I be confused when *he* asked *me* to go with him to the grocery store and instead took me on a drive around the cornfields late into the night?

How could I be confused when he told me he could see himself falling for me?

"I'm going to head to bed." Liam gets to his feet and ambles toward the door. I can feel his eyes on me as he looks back, but I don't dare meet his tortured gaze. "I'm sorry, Callie."

"Just go," I say in a cold voice choked with sorrow.

Liam stands outside the front door for a long moment before disappearing inside.

I decide faster than the door can swing close that I will not mourn the loss of him. So much for older men being more mature.

No. I am going to fucking live. I'm going to grow up. Fast.

I crush the flowers in my hands, feeling the sticky insides of their stems and petals ooze.

———◆O◆———

Present day...

Pounding on the door. "Callie! What the hell are you doing in there?!"

I snap out of my trance. "Sorry! One more minute!"

"You said that five minutes ago."

I don't reply, balling my hand into a fist, watching the veins beneath the tattoo bulge slightly. When the tattoo doesn't serve as a memory, it's a reminder. Be tender and take no shit.

Especially from your older brother's best friends.

"I'm coming in!"

The door flies open, but I catch it with my hands, shoving it closed.

"I'm naked!"

"I don't care!"

I grab my towel, pull it around me, and open the door for Sasha. "All yours."

"Finally!" Sasha pushes past me. "Ugh, you soaked the bathmat."

I sigh. It's just going to be one of those days.

Chapter 2

Callie

My new client is sending a car to pick me up for my first day of work. That way, I can transport my luggage and everything I'll need for my time as his caregiver. The driver is very kind and doesn't let me lift a finger when it comes to my two suitcases, plus my medical kit.

I'm on pins and needles to find out who this guy actually is. I don't want to be taken off-guard if it's some celebrity I recognize. I'm hoping it's someone in finance I'd never be able to identify at first glance.

Brooklyn glides by as we make our way into Manhattan.

Partway through our drive, my phone rings.

Nate. My brother. I pick up whenever he calls, mostly because his schedule is so hectic when he's out on the rig I don't know the next time I'll hear from him.

"Hello?" I answer.

"Don't pick up like you don't know it's me."

"Sorry, who is this?"

"You're such an ass," Nate says through a laugh.

"Ah, the only person who calls me an ass is my older brother. Is this him?"

Nate continues to laugh on the other end of the phone. "You *know* it's me, Callie."

I smile to myself and sink deeper into the plush leather interior of the car, casting a look out at the city flashing by. "How's it goin', Natey?"

"Oh, who cares how I'm doing?! How are *you* doing? Miss First-Day-On-The-Job?"

I giggle. "I'm doing well. Nervous."

"Bah! What for? You're going to be amazing. Your client is going to love you, and if he doesn't, he's an idiot."

"Okay, not the best attitude to have going into this, but I'll take it."

"You have to call me and tell me all about it when you get settled. I just got home so you'll have no problem reaching me the next couple of weeks."

I smile to myself. Nate is still working on the same rig. He's worked his way up to head engineer and still loves it, which blows my mind. Being stranded at sea on a giant piece of machinery isn't my idea of a good time, but it works for him. "How are the girls?"

"Good. We're going to be celebrating second Christmas in a couple days."

I don't know how he handles missing holidays and events for this job, but he makes it work. The credit really goes to his wife, Felicity, who holds down the fort while he's gone. With two young daughters and a full-time job as a hotel manager, she's a superhero. Since Nate was on the rig this past Christmas, they're making up for it even though it's already January.

"Send me pictures once you decorate the tree."

"And *you* have to send me pics of your new digs! Seriously, Cal, you'll probably be in the lap of luxury."

We've hit Midtown by now. The buildings are getting taller, the traffic getting denser. "We'll see. You know how rich people are. Unexpectedly cheap when it comes to the most important things."

"Oh, come on, be optimistic."

I won't admit it, but I am. I've had dreams about a view of Central Park, chef-cooked meals, fresh flowers, silk sheets... my mind has run wild with thoughts of how my new employer might take care of me. I know I'm getting ahead of myself; I'll just be an employee in their home. Not a family member. Not a friend.

A girl can dream, can't she?

"I'll send you pictures when I get a chance."

"Great."

"Say hi to Felicity! And Stella and Vivi."

"Hey!" Nate shouts away from the phone. "Aunt California says hi!"

I hear some echoing "hellos" from the girls through the phone and laugh at their nickname for me. Callie really is short for Callista, but I've never gone by that in my life. Sounds too old-fashioned and grandmotherly. Callie suits me just fine.

"Love you, Natey."

"You too, sis. Be good."

I chuckle and hang up the phone. I've always been the good kid in the family. Nate was the wild one. We joke that's why Mom and Dad had me so long after he was born, to get a second crack at things. But we both turned out good for the most part, I think.

We've reached the thick of the Upper East Side, on renowned Fifth Avenue. I'm stunned when the car pulls up in front of a towering building that looks to be Art Deco in design. I can't even move a muscle before my car door opens. I pull my purse into my lap tightly and look up at the doorman. He looks to be in his fifties, with cheeks burnt red from the winter wind, yet he smiles jovially. "We've been expecting you."

"You have?" I ask weakly.

"Yes!" He holds out his hand and helps me out of the car. "I'm Frederick, the doorman. And while I know you're a guest of Mr. Sterling, I have no idea who you might be."

Mr. Sterling... that name alone sounds expensive.

"I'm Callie. Callie Emerson."

"Ms. Emerson, it's a pleasure to make your acquaintance."

"Yours as well. But please, just call me Callie."

Frederick chuckles. "I'm afraid we're under strict guidelines to call our guests by their formal names. But I'll keep it in mind, Ms. Emerson."

He starts to pull me away from the car. "Oh, my bags, I've got things in the –"

"Don't you worry about that. That's all taken care of."

I glance over my shoulder at the trunk of the car. The driver and another man clad in the same blue coat Frederick is wearing are pulling my bags out with care.

This is oddly a trial by fire. I'm not used to being waited on like this. And I'm not sure if I like it.

"Welcome to The Conrad, your home for the next few months," Frederick announces, gesturing toward the ornate lobby as we walk through the automatic sliding doors.

The luxurious interior leaves me gob-smacked with its marble floors, velvet lounge chairs and gold-plated elevators. This is beyond my wildest dreams.

"Now, I'm going to send you up to the penthouse" Frederick says, leading me to the elevator. He presses the "up" button and then smiles at me. "Your bags will be brought up and delivered to your room at Mr. Sterling's direction."

The doors open. That was impossibly fast.

"If you have any questions or concerns during your stay, don't hesitate to contact me." Frederick pulls a business card out of his coat and hands it to me. It has his name and lists multiple phone numbers on how to reach him.

"Thank you, Frederick."

He holds the elevator door for me and ushers me through. "It's my pleasure, Ms. Emerson."

Once I'm inside, he presses the penthouse button for me and then steps back. With a small nod and a wink, Frederick disappears as the doors shut.

The elevator heaves upward and my heart starts to jump out of my chest. What the hell have I gotten myself into? I know I left hospitals for a reason, but this is a complete culture shock. No more being cajoled out of the shower by Sasha or praying that the furnace doesn't give out in the middle of the night.

No, this is the lap of luxury.

After an impossibly quick ride, I'm at the top floor, the penthouse. I step off into a small hallway. There's no way I could get lost as there's one singular door opposite me. Dark, cherry wood is adorned with a gold door knocker and matching peephole. I glance around to see if there's a doorbell, but no such luck.

Knocker it is.

I reach for the gold door knocker in the shape of a ring in the center of the lion's mouth. I feel like I'm in a Grimm Brothers fairytale just looking at it.

Before my hand reaches it, though, the door flies open, and a woman appears. She is young with a peppy smile and olive skin. I'm surprised that her attire is so casual: a tank top and slouchy jeans. Clearly, Mr. Sterling isn't too keen on a dress code. "Are you the nurse?"

"Yes, that's me."

"Hi, I'm Emma." She holds out her hand and we shake. "I'm Mr. Sterling's housekeeper."

Ah, so Mr. Sterling is *that* kind of rich. "Pleased to meet you."

"Well, come on in, don't be shy!" Emma says, gesturing to me to come inside.

I follow Emma into the foyer. The interior of the penthouse doesn't quite match the ornate lobby. It's a different sort of luxury. Dark wood, crisp lines, leather.

A man lives here.

Along the walls are different posters of book covers. All are written by the same man. *Liam Sterling.*

Holy shit. Liam Sterling has become the equivalent of James Patterson in the crime fiction world. I don't read the genre myself, but it's hard to go anywhere without seeing his name plastered on billboards. Not to mention he's so reclusive hardly anyone knows his face.

No wonder they wanted to keep him anonymous.

Emma takes my coat and puts it in the closet off the foyer, which looks more like a whole coat check than a closet. "We've all been so excited to meet you..." She pauses. "I'm afraid I don't know your name yet. The agency was very clear about the required anonymity."

I smile. I'm glad it works both ways. It's more fair that way. "Callie Emerson."

"Callie. That's a beautiful name."

"Oh, thanks."

"If you'll follow me into the living room, I'll introduce you to Mr. Sterling."

My heart begins to pound again as I follow her through the foyer. A doorway to the left leads to a state-of-the-art kitchen and then, the hallway opens into a dining room that transitions into the living room. Very modern. No privacy. The dining table is covered in various papers and a laptop poised at the head.

To the left, the living room is sort of in shambles. Furniture has been pushed out of the way and the carpet rolled up in order to allow for easier access. This is helpful considering my client, who is sitting facing away from me and looking out the windows, is in a wheelchair due to an accident.

He is accompanied by a man who is standing by, holding a steaming up of something. "Cup of tea for you, the way you like it."

"Mmh. Thank you," Sterling grumbles.

From the back, I can tell this man is in need of help. His dark brown hair is overgrown, and his clothing looks extremely wrinkled. He probably hasn't changed in several days.

The man with the tea, a beanpole with ash gray hair, deposits the drink on a tray near the chair, then looks up at me and Emma. "Is this her?"

"Yes. Mr. Sterling, Wade... allow me to introduce you to Callie. Or do you prefer to go by nurse Emerson?" Emma asks with a concerned look.

Mr. Sterling sits up straight in his chair, perking up at the sound of my name. Must be a good sign.

I smile at Emma. "Callie is just fine. Perfect, actually."

"I'm Wade. I cook the food and make the tea around here," Wade says in a chipper tone.

"Callie Emerson, hm?"

We all look at Mr. Sterling. He hasn't bothered to turn around or to look at me.

"Yes, Mr. Sterling. But if you're alright with it, you can just call me Callie."

I watch his shoulders rise and fall as he breathes. What's wrong with him? Is he some eccentric, tyrannical, artist type?

"Wade, turn me around," Mr. Sterling says curtly.

Wade hurriedly follows the instruction with a murmured apology.

And as soon as Mr. Sterling is turned around, my heart drops.

I know him.

I know him so well my heart aches.

It's been ten years, but I could recognize him anywhere because of his amber eyes. Even through a veil of messy hair and scruff teetering into beard territory covers his face, I know him.

Liam. Love of my little humdrum hometown life Liam.

Back then, he was Liam Kaminsky.

Now he's...

Liam Sterling.

And I'm his nurse.

Chapter 3

Liam

Callie Emerson. I'd doubted I'd ever see her again.

I try to hold back the shock on my face, but it's hard when faced with a part of my past I'm not proud of. I've carried the wound of hurting Callie with me all these ten years.

We're both different now. I'm certainly different, no longer on the rig, a crime writer with billions of dollars. Not to mention now I'm in a wheelchair. Temporarily.

And Callie, well... time's been good to her.

Her blonde hair that was short and wild back in the day falls in silky tresses down to her shoulders. She's grown up, and grown into the curves of her body. She doesn't hold herself so shyly anymore. Head high, strong jaw. A nurse.

My nurse.

Holy shit.

I just realized I haven't said anything since turning around to face her. My eyes have just been locked in her blue stare like I've been trapped in an iceberg. "Um – uh... hello."

If I had only known, I would have maybe shaved or gotten my hair trimmed or something.

Oh, who am I kidding? If I had known that Callie was going to be my nurse, I would have stopped that from happening at the outset.

"It's nice to meet you," I say with a definitive tone. No need to let everyone in on our past. It's not personal. Just business.

Callie's eyes widen slightly, only because I'm looking for it. "You as well, Mr. Sterling," she says with coldness.

In my head, I'm running through every solution to this issue I possibly can. I could ask the agency for a new nurse. But that feels wrong. It doesn't feel right to have Callie here, but it doesn't feel right to cast her aside either.

I knew she was living in New York, and I knew she'd finished up her nursing degree. But that was the extent of what Nate told me. God, when was the last time I talked to him? Months ago now. I'm not the best at keeping in touch. My schedule keeps me busy. If it weren't for the accident, I'd be moving a mile a minute. But my latest project has grounded to a halt given the weakness in my legs and the tingling nerves in my right hand. It might not be broken, but I can barely use it.

"Why don't you tell Callie about what happened to you, Mr. Sterling?" Emma encourages with wide eyes.

I toss my hand in her direction. "You do it." I can't be bothered. I'm still reeling over the fact that Callie fucking Emerson is standing in my living room and will be living in my house for the next three months to take care of me.

Karma's a bitch, isn't it?

Although, to be fair to myself, I think I did the right thing. There was no way that Callie and I could have kept up our innocent affair once Nate and I went back to the rig. On top of that, she was only eighteen and I was a full decade older than her. That's an age gap if I ever heard of one. She needed time to grow up.

Maybe I was a coward. I really cared for her. But the two of us made no sense. Especially with her brother involved.

When Nate invited me home from the rig for our month break around the fourth of July, he had made the invitation on one condition. "Don't so much as even *think* about looking at my sister."

"'Course not, man," I remember replying. "She's just a kid. I'm not that type of guy."

It only took two days for me to become that type of guy. Callie consumed my heart and soul from the first time I saw her.

She was the most dangerous angel I had ever met.

Now, here I am at the mercy of her care.

"Mr. Sterling was in a skiing accident," Emma says, her slight Bronx accent coming through. She goes to the dining table and picks up a file of papers she's collected about my case. I don't know what I'd do without her. She was a house-keeper, manager and laundress extraordinaire. "You can see all the details of his injuries here."

Callie takes it cautiously and pulls out a pair of reading glasses from her purse, her eyes snapping to me for a split second.

We've both gotten older, that's for sure. Callie's lived some more life; I've completely changed mine. And now she wears reading glasses.

It'd be kind of cute if this whole situation wasn't so messed up.

"Mm..." she hums, perusing the documents. "Partial paralysis, huh?"

"Just for a few days. Waist down. It went away, but it's left him very weak since he got home."

Callie looks to me again, this time to my hand. "And the hand?"

"Stiff beyond belief! But not broken!" Emma says with a giggle. She doesn't always have the best-timed cheerfulness. "He's been doing some exercises for it, but it's kept him from writing."

Callie shrugs. "Dictation software is –"

"Crap," I interject crudely. I clear my throat. "Never knows what the hell I'm saying or where the commas go. It's shit."

The room is silent. I don't care if I sound like a curmudgeon. I know I'm turning into more of one by the day. I'm almost forty for crying out loud. This accident has aged me at least ten years. Who knows how long until I need a walker or cane?

"I see," Callie says, pursing her lips. She flips through a few more documents before snapping the folder closed and smiling proudly. "Well, you've come to the right place. Rehabilitation is a long, but necessary journey."

"We just loved your file. Wade and I, that is."

Wade nods eagerly.

I'm starting to wonder if maybe I should have been the one looking through the files. I certainly wouldn't have chosen a young woman, regardless of if I knew her or not. I don't need that kind of distraction in my life while I'm cooped up like this.

"Perhaps Mr. Sterling and I could have a moment alone together and discuss a treatment plan for the next three months," Callie says, eyes zeroing in on me.

Oo... she looks mad. The only times I've seen her mad were when she was losing at Taboo while we played it with her family.

No matter. I'm in charge here. I've got her like a puppet on a string when it comes to her paycheck. I know very few people who would refuse a contract like the one she's received.

"That's alright with me as long as it's alright with Mr. Ster—"

"More than alright with me. Let's take our meeting in the library, shall we?"

Callie tries not to look surprised, but I suspect she's known few if any people with a library in their home.

Wade reaches for my chair, but I roll away from him. "I've got it, I've got it."

I roll myself out of the living room, into the hall, and through the tight doorway of the library. I've gotten pretty good at handling this thing. However, though the chair allows me to use just one hand, it can make my arm extremely tired.

For Callie's sake, though, I'm not willing to look weak.

I turn my chair around to face a leather armchair, one I've spent many nights reading and writing in over the years I've lived in the penthouse.

Callie appears in the doorway, lingering as if she's a vampire needing to be invited inside.

"Sit," I say with a nod toward the chair. "And close the door first."

She follows my directions and sits down in the seat across from me.

I purse my lips and stare at her. I will not be the first to speak.

Callie doesn't need to be goaded though. "I wish I could say it's good to see you, Liam, but..."

Ouch. That cut to the quick. "The feeling is mutual."

"Is that why you pretended not to recognize me?" Her eyes flash anger at me. "That was a low blow."

I'm rendered silent. Callie looks out the bay window, taking steady breaths. "I'm sorry, I was... taken off-guard," I offer.

"So was I."

"Really?"

She glares. "Of course. I had no idea who you were. Even if I had known your name, I wouldn't have known it was *the* Liam Kaminsky." My name comes out of her mouth with vitriol. I guess it's true what they say - the first cut is the deepest.

"I never thought I'd see you again either, Callie. I mean, that was ten years ago."

Callie swallows. "I guess we were different people then."

"Guess so."

We are both silent again.

"Alright, well. What do you wanna do? You want a new client? Or are you willing to stick it out with me?"

Callie raises an eyebrow. "You want me to be your nurse?"

"Well..." The answer is not "no," but it's not "yes" either. "Look, you were the highest recommended rehabilitation nurse at your firm. According to Emma. And I need to get back to normal as fast as possible. I don't want to be stuck in this chair a second longer than I have to be. So, would you help me?"

She considers for a long moment, leaving me on edge. I'm half expecting for her to reject me just as I did her all those years ago. Then, she smiles, "I guess it's been so long we barely even know each other anymore. So, what's the harm?"

Damn, Callie has learned the art of the cutting remark. I'll have to keep that for one of my books. "Great."

"Great." She slaps her thighs and stands. "I think I'm going to get settled. Then we can talk about your treatment plan, hm?"

"Sounds good..."

Callie crosses to the door, but as soon as she touches the handle, I stop her.

"And Callie? Let's keep you and me between you and me? Get my meaning?"

She gives me a bitter smile with narrow eyes. "As far as I know there was no 'you and me.' Not really."

Then, she disappears through the door.

And I'm left with a hollowness deep inside me where the memory of Callie has been living, now knowing that she absolutely hates my guts.

Chapter 4

Callie

Though I verbally agreed to stay with Liam, there's not an ice cube's chance in hell I'm not gonna try and get out of here.

Unfortunately, that doesn't seem like it's going to be easy.

"I'm sorry, Callie, but without a strong reason, I'm afraid we can't just place you with a new client in the blink of an eye," my boss, Polly, says over the phone.

I sigh and fall back into the pillows. I had a fitful night of sleep despite the bed being lush and cozy. Much better than the pullout couch I was sleeping on at Sasha's.

Today is my first day of physical therapy with Liam. And I'm dreading it. I spent most of yesterday learning the ropes regarding the penthouse from Wade and Emma. Thank God they're here, because if it was just Liam and I, I might lose my mind.

He's changed. He's no longer the smooth-voiced gentleman, but a misanthrope who never even smiles and who needs a bath.

I don't doubt he's suffered. Partial paralysis, even if temporary, can be traumatic. Not just to the body, but to the mind. The idea that you may not move again has to be terrifying.

That doesn't mean he gets to be an ass about it, though.

However, this is how he's always been according to Emma.

"Oh, that's just Mr. Sterling," she had said with a giggle when I mentioned how surly he seemed.

Not to mention... Mr. Sterling? Is he serious making people call him that? Has he forgotten his roots? He worked on an oil rig and came from blue collar stock. How can he just abandon all that?

Needless to say, I want out.

"I just think there is probably a nurse who is a better match for Mr. Sterling," I say into the phone in a low voice.

Polly huffs. "Like I said, it's not that easy. And I would need Mr. Sterling's approval if I was going to give him another nurse."

I swallow. I know what she means. Unless I completely fabricate something, there's no reason for me to be placed with someone else. And while I've grown into a strong woman, I don't have a lot of gumption to lie. "Sure, I understand."

"And most of our clients are pretty demanding."

"It's not that he's demanding, it's –"

"All I'm saying is that by working in this field, in this particular job, you might come up against people who... act in a way that you find intolerable." I hear what she's saying. Money talks. And she's right. "But you've got to learn to tolerate it. I'll make a note that if a better fit comes along, you want to be considered. But for now, Callie, do the job. I know you can."

I nod. "Thanks, Polly."

The call ends and I'm left alone in the early morning light of my room. It's a beautiful room, that's for sure. I sent Nate just a couple pictures, the ones that wouldn't tip him off that this was Liam's house. There's no way I can tell him. I've kept the secret of our affair this long and, I don't know what it would do to me if Nate knew that Liam was back in my life. I wouldn't be able to keep it in anymore. So, he got to see my bathroom, complete with heated toilet seat, and my big closet which currently just houses my scrubs.

"Okay, Callie. Big day. You got this," I say as an encouragement to get myself out of bed. It doesn't work. The thought of facing Liam again curdles my brain. I wonder if he still sees that little girl, he left behind in Indiana. The one with the freshly picked daisies in her hand.

"Ughhhh," I groan and fall back into the pillows.

Five more minutes can't hurt.

———◄O►———

I should have slept in more than five minutes. We're going on eleven in the morning and still Liam hasn't stirred. I've been sitting in the living room with my equipment all set up for us to do some physical therapy, sinking deeper and deeper into the couch.

"You sure you don't want something to eat, Callie?"

I look up at Wade. I had told him I don't eat breakfast, but now, for my schedule, we're closing in on lunch. "Ah, what the hell. Sure."

He hands me the prettiest bowl of oatmeal I've ever seen, adorned in berries and cream.

"Wow. That's beautiful." I take a spoonful. The flavors meld together on my tongue. "Thank you."

Wade grins. "Sorry that he's kept you waiting."

I'm trying not to devour the oats, but I'm ravenous. "It's okay. He told me he'd be up early."

"Ha! That's classic Sterling."

I raise an eyebrow.

"He thinks he's a morning person, but I've only seen him out of bed before nine a handful of times."

Great. So, he's rich and wastes people's time. How original.

"Are you talking about me?"

Wade and I both turn to find Liam haphazardly strewn in his chair, rolling into the room.

"Jesus, Liam, you should have called me," I say as I stand.

"I can get out of bed, Callie," he says with an aggravated look in his eye.

I look him over skeptically. Sure, he made it into the chair, but his appearance is sloppy and his clothes are stretched from struggling to get comfortable. I know he can stand, and he apparently can walk too, but there's no reason for him to do things just because he can.

"Breakfast, Mr. Sterling?" Wade asks.

"Please," his boss grunts, rolling up to the only spot at the table that isn't covered in documents or random nonsense.

"Paper for you on the table," Wade calls over his shoulder as he skitters out of the room.

I go over toward the table, eating the oatmeal as I go. I haven't been invited to sit, so I opt to hover instead.

"Are you just going to stand there?" Liam asks, voice brittle and dry from sleep.

"Um. No, I can sit."

"What a talent," he murmurs as I sit a few seats down from him.

We are both silent. *Awkward.* In the kitchen, I can hear clanking pans and the sizzle of something. *Mmm...bacon.*

"You've got something on your..." Liam gestures to his neckline and then to me.

I look down and find a clump of oatmeal on my scrub top. "Oh. Oops." I wipe it away, trying not to die of embarrassment.

"Do you always wear scrubs?"

"Well, kinda. It's my job."

"But you're not in a hospital."

I want to melt into the floor and never be seen again. There's no reason I should need to defend myself to him and yet he terrifies me. "They're comfortable."

"Mm." Liam reaches for the newspaper and starts to unfold it.

I let him read for a few moments before clearing my throat.

"You want to say something?"

"Well, just... after your breakfast, we should do some exercises."

Liam's eyes scan the living room. "Jesus, you have the parallel bars here and everything."

I glance over at the bars I use to help my clients gain strength while walking. They take up most of the living room, but luckily fold up into mostly nothing. "Yes, I think that –"

"I don't need those."

"Sorry?"

"I'm not like…I can walk."

I hold back a scoff. "It's just to help get you stronger."

"I'm not actually paralyzed, I'm just weak."

This guy can't be serious. Just yesterday, he was saying how he wants to get better as quickly as possible. "They're going to help a lot if you just –"

"No. I'll pass."

I go quiet. Liam's fiery eyes stick in mine. I can't believe I'm looking at the same man I once adored with all my heart. He's changed. But I can't afford to fight him on this. For now, I'll let it slide. "Fine. We can do chair exercises once you're finished eating."

⋯⋯◄O►⋯⋯

The exercise goes about as poorly as that conversation did. He is obstinate, cynical, and I despise him. It's like he's trying to make things hard for me.

After only a half hour of exercises, Liam declares he's done for the day and retreats to the library. Fine with me. I stay out of his way, spending my time either talking with Emma and Wade, or keeping to my damn self. The only other duty I have is to manage his pain meds. At least until he stops being a dick.

If this is what the next three months will be, so be it.

I take my dinner alone in my room. There was nothing in my contract about spending time with the client. I'll just do the work and that's it.

Emma and Wade are gone by nine, leaving a very empty, very huge penthouse to just Liam and me.

I decide to turn in early, take a shower, put on my pajamas, and just sleep off this disaster of a day, but the second I tuck under the covers, I hear Liam cry for me.

"Callie! Callie, come quick!"

I leap out of bed and down the hallway to the living room where Liam is rolling his chair back and forth as if he's pacing. "What is it? What's wrong?"

"Go over there," he says, snapping his fingers toward the laptop.

"What? Why? Are you hurt?" I start to go toward him.

Liam shakes his head. "No, I need you to sit down and write for me."

My eyes widen. "What?"

"I need you to –"

"I heard you," I cut him off. If he repeats it, I'm afraid steam will pour out of my ears. "Liam, I'm not here to... be dictated to. I'm not even here to talk with you. I'm here to take care of you."

Liam lowers his chin, still looking at me with a dark gaze. He holds up his bad hand. "I can't write, Callie."

I shiver when he says my name. Not in a good way.

"And I'm a writer. You see how that could be a problem, couldn't you?"

Jesus Christ, is this guy serious?

"If it's your job to take care of me –"

"Your *health,* Liam. Not your books!"

"—then, you should take care of me."

A standoff. Our eyes locked in one another's. The last time this happened, he broke my heart.

This time, I'd love to break his neck.

Too bad I'm a nurse. Should have gone into a different business for that.

"Callie..." Liam jerks his head toward the laptop. "Quickly. Before my inspiration runs out."

I clench my fists at my sides. I know what children are like. You say yes to them once and you have to say yes forever. Well, Liam, despite his "maturity" and age, is just a petulant child.

And I'm at his godforsaken mercy.

"Just this once," I say through gritted teeth. "But under one condition."

"I don't do that sort of thing."

Ignoring him, I say, "Tomorrow, you'll try the parallel bars. Or I'm walking out that door right now."

Liam smirks. "You wouldn't."

"Like hell I wouldn't," I say with spitfire venom, faster than I can even think.

He pauses. I've surprised him.

Good.

"Fine. Deal. Now, do you mind? When inspiration strikes it's like an hourglass. Go, go."

I follow his instructions and go to sit at the head of the table where the laptop is.

"Chapter fourteen."

"I'm not ready."

"*Chapter fourteen.*"

I could strangle him. But the deal has been made. I type as fast as I can.

"*Millie woke up in a cold sweat. She knew she wasn't alone. Was it just the cat or something more sinister?*"

I nearly laugh. Is this really the kind of thing people like to read? This is what has made Liam Sterling *billions* of dollars. Shit, I picked the wrong career.

However, it doesn't take long for me to realize why Liam is the master. He starts to unwind the story with his words so easily, I find myself engrossed, losing speed as I type.

That voice that was so gruff is now turning into the buttery smoothness I once knew. Though I can't look at him, his voice takes me back, if only for a moment.

Three months of this.

I'll make it work.

Chapter 5

Liam

"Easy... take it easy..."

I grip the parallel bar tight with my good hand. My stiff one manages as best it can. I take it slow.

"Good, you can put a little more weight on this leg." Callie gestures to the outside of my right thigh. For a split second, I think she's about to touch me and I get goosebumps.

Take it easy, Kaminsky.

I follow her instructions, taking my next step with my right leg. The extra bit of weight proves too much for my knee and it gives out just a bit. I cling onto the bar and Callie grabs my shoulder. "You alright?"

There's her hand right there on my arm. Feels like it could burn me. "Yeah. Yeah, I'm fine." I pull my arm away from her. I can't have her touching me like that. It brings back too many memories.

Callie and I might never have gone to bed together, but we did so many other things. I remember the feeling of her hand in mine, her legs draped over my lap, our fully clothed bodies lying together in the dewy field at daybreak.

For her, it was young love. For me, it was... a fluke.

"You want to stop?" Callie asks, her blue eyes looking at me like a teacher asking a math problem.

"Um. Yeah. Sure. Just for a moment." It's a bit embarrassing for her to see me like this. Being able to walk and function as I always have is something I should have been more grateful for.

Callie positions my chair at the end of the bars. I make my way over and start to sink down. She puts her hands under my arms and guides me down into it. I'm suddenly hyper aware that I need a shower. I must stink.

After all these years, Callie sees me for the first time and I've got weak legs, a bum hand, and I smell bad.

Tough break.

"Maybe we can try eating again," Callie says softly.

I groan. "No, not hungry today."

She grabs the back of my chair. "You need your strength, Liam."

I sigh.

"Can I move you?"

It's sweet she always asks for consent. Emma and Wade aren't always so good about that. They'll jostle me a bit out of the way or roll me in the wrong direction. Callie always asks. And I've given her enough reason to not be so respectful by being an ass.

"Fine. But I'm not eating."

Callie laughs. "Okay, Liam." She rolls me back over to the dining table where we were sitting earlier before we started our exercises. A plate of cold food sits at my place. Before I can say anything, she snatches it away and disappears into the hall. "Let me heat this up."

"I'm not eating!"

"Yes, you are!"

I smile to myself but drop it immediately.

No smiling. No laughing. She's your nurse, not your friend.

I haven't been able to avoid remembering. Since the very first day she walked in here, I've had scourges of memories, sometimes waking, sometimes sleeping.

And I can't say I'm upset about them.

It just makes it hard to face her after I've had a memory of tenderly kissing whipped cream off her lips in the kitchen of her childhood home while all her family was just in the next room.

I've experienced love since Callie. Or things like it. But nothing quite as pure as that.

It'd be foolish to believe that anything between us would be like that again. For one, she hates my guts. Unless we're working on something to do with my condition, she ignores me, barely glancing my way. For the other... we're older. Some may say wiser, but I'd say we're both more hardened to the world. We've both been hurt.

I know I was her first hurt. And being here must be painful for her.

I wouldn't dare bring it up, though.

"Here we are!" Callie announces and puts the plate down in front of me again. The scent of steaming broccoli, salmon, and rice hit my nose and I hold my breath to keep from gagging.

I cover my mouth. "Really, Callie, I can't even think about eating."

Callie sinks into her usual spot, two over from me. "Liam, if you want to get stronger faster, you have to try." She smiles solemnly. "Please."

"Dammit, I'm not eating. You can't make me. I'm not a child."

"I know that. If you were, I'd be giving you a spoonful of pureed peas and pretending like it was a plane zooming into your mouth."

I glance over at her and try not to laugh. "Fine. You have a point."

Callie rests her elbows on the table, her chin in her palms. Right there, I can see the girl she used to be, so innocent with her hair tied back in a ponytail off her face. She's lost some of the baby fat in her cheeks, showing off her svelte cheekbones.

She could have been a model. I'm sure of it.

"Tell you what."

"What?" I ask, now squeezing my nose so I don't get even the slightest whiff of salmon.

She smiles sweetly. "Let's play a little game."

"Oh God."

"For each bite you take, you can ask me a question about my life."

I raise an eyebrow.

"And for each bite you refuse. I can ask you one."

"Really, Callie, this isn't some getting to know you thing. This is –"

"Aren't you curious?" she asks. It's not judgmental. It's genuine. "Because I'm really curious what you've done over the past ten years to get you…" She glances around at the expanse of the penthouse. "Here."

I nod slowly. She's not wrong. I am curious. What's her life like outside of here? Her family. Her friends. Boyfriend? That thought shouldn't make me jealous but it does. "Okay, fine." I remove my hand from my mouth and clench my good hand around the fork. "One bite. One question." I scoop up some rice and broccoli, leaving the pungent salmon for later, and swallow it down fast. It hits my stomach like a stone. "Ugh. Fine. So…"

Callie cocks her head to the side. "So…"

Think, Liam, think. "Um. How was school?"

Callie's eyebrows jump and she lets out a loud laugh. "Who are you? My dad?"

"Don't be mean. I couldn't think of anything else."

Callie keeps laughing until it peters out and she sighs. "That was a good one." She flicks a few tears of laughter out from under her eyes. "It was good."

"You owe me more of an answer than that."

"Well, I'm here, aren't I? Not just anyone can be a personal nurse to the rich and famous, Liam."

I purse my lips. I've worked hard to get where I am but being called "rich and famous" doesn't sit well in my stomach, even though I'm objectively both.

"Is that satisfactory?"

No. "Sure."

"Another bite…" she says in a sing-song voice.

It's only fair to let her ask a question too. Besides, I'd be interested to know what she wants to know about me. She might go right for the jugular, drag us into the past and her heartache, but one thing about me is I don't mind playing with fire from time to time. "No. You can ask a question."

Callie eyes me. "Fine. How'd this all happen?"

I frown.

She gestures to the penthouse, her fingers dotting the air like she's bestowing glimmering magic around the room. "All this. Last I knew, you were an oil rig worker trying to pay off your student loans."

I hum thoughtfully. "Well, hit my big break, I guess."

"More..."

"I'm getting there, I'm getting there." She's always been curious. I think that's why we gravitated toward one another. I, the writer, always looking at the world for another story. And she, at the time, was young and vibrant. Wondering what life had in store. It's good she hasn't lost that spirit. "Well. I sold a story. And then another one. Then I had a publisher. Then it was four books a year and it's been that way ever since. Movie deals. Scripts. You name it. This..." I look around the penthouse. It's much more luxurious than the bungalow I grew up in, that's for sure. "Just a by-product of that."

"Jeez, how do you keep up with that work?"

I chuckle. "That's another question."

Callie smiles. "Ahh... you want to play that way, huh? Fine. Another bite. You can ask another question."

I take another bite of the food and force it down my gullet. "So. Your life. You came to New York for school."

"Yes..."

"Stayed in New York for work..."

"Mhm..."

"So, what's your life look like now? If you're so willing to waste three months of your life trapped here with me?"

Callie nods. "Yes, it is a bit masochistic, isn't it?"

"Hey!"

"Don't act like you weren't thinking it."

"Just because I was thinking it, doesn't mean I want it to be true," I say measuredly. She might be an unwelcome surprise in my life. But each passing day I yearn for that month we had ten years ago.

Callie's smile drops slightly. She shakes her head as if she had a response she's not sharing. Damn. Wish I knew what she was thinking, if only for a second. "Um. Well. If you recall, I wasn't willing to spend three months trapped here with *you* specifically, but I guess that's the hand I've been dealt."

I don't reply. My bum hand is starting to tingle. I try to squeeze it underneath the table, but the joints are stiffening.

"It's good money. Three months of my life isn't so bad, as long as you keep cooperating."

"So, there's nothing you're missing? Out there?"

"I'm not trapped here, you know. It's not *Jane Eyre.* I'm not stuck out on the moors or something."

I nod. "I know, but when you spend six days a week on call and get one day off... I just wonder what you're missing."

Callie folds her hands under her chin and watches me for a moment before nodding to my plate. "That's another bite, I'd say."

I follow her instructions. Another bite. Another forced swallow.

Callie looks off across the penthouse with a contemplative gaze. "I don't feel like I'm missing much. Sure, New York is big and loud and sometimes it makes me feel lost. I like having a purpose. I like knowing what's coming next. Even if you've thrown quite a wrench into my plans."

"Have I?" I say with a chuckle.

"That's another question."

"Now you're just being pedantic."

She giggles. The sound gives me déjà vu. It brings me right back to a moment of her shy laughter when I first told her she was beautiful.

The compliment still stands.

"Fine. You ask a question."

"Alright. What about you? What are you missing being all cooped up?" Callie asks. "You must live a pretty amazing life. Skiing and... things."

I laugh loudly. "Skiing and things, huh? Is that all you see in me?"

"I don't know. With all the money in the world, you must do a lot of cool things."

I have done a lot of "cool things." I travel and have adventures across the globe. Most of the time, though, I'm traveling for work, for research, because there's some expectation on me. The adventurousness of my youth, the reason I was on an oil rig has lost its purity. My impulses are stifled by work. And frankly, so is my creativity.

But it's gotten me this far.

"Yeah. I've had to cancel a few trips. Meetings. My book is on hold. Until now. Thanks to you."

Callie looks at the laptop. "If you think I'm typing for you again –"

"Think again, I know." I'll get her to type again. My volatile artist nature always gets its way.

Callie runs her hand through her blonde hair and takes in a deep breath. Her chest rises. Even under her burgundy scrubs, the outline of her breasts makes me weak.

Before I left her, I had my chance. I knew she wanted her first time to be with me. I couldn't bring myself to do it, though. It wouldn't be right to make love to her and then walk away. I've always been curious though who got the honor of being Callie Emerson's first. I drag my fork around my plate and pick up a huge bite. Chew it up, swallow it down. "My turn."

"Alright."

"Do you have a boyfriend?"

"No."

Another bite.

"Girlfriend?"

"No."

Another bite.

"Have you ever?"

Callie hesitates. "Yes."

I gobble up some more food.

"Liam, slow down, you don't want to –"

"Did you let them make love to you?"

Callie's blue eyes widen. Her pupils like pinpricks. I know immediately I shouldn't have asked.

But I need to know.

"I'm a twenty-eight-year-old woman."

"What's that supposed to mean?"

"Obviously, Liam." She pushes herself up, her chair squealing angrily underneath her. "Obviously I didn't wait for you."

Callie stomps off to her quarters, slamming the door behind her.

I'm left with a plate of half-eaten food and the deep regret that her first time hadn't been with me.

Chapter 6

Callie

Liam has not let me give him a bath since I've arrived. He's been adamant he can do it himself, but when I'm close to him, helping with his rehab, he's starting to smell stale.

I don't blame him for keeping me at arm's length. Why should we be closer than we already are?

However, each passing day makes it harder for me to avoid wanting to be close to Liam again. Through his "tough guy" exterior, I've had glimpses of the man I knew ten years ago - soft smiles, goofy jokes, a light tease here and there.

Of course, this is all dependent on how he's feeling on a given day. And whoever said artists are temperamental was right. Liam is a textbook case.

However, I can be temperamental too. Today, I've refused to do our rehab exercises unless Liam lets me give him a bath. This is for no other reason than not wanting a nose full of body odor. I know that a bath means that Liam will be naked, but I promise to all that is holy that it's not even a tertiary motivation for getting him cleaned.

The bath is all prepared, filled to the brim with bubbles so there's no possibility that under the water I'll get an eyeful of Liam's groin. Other than that, I just have to keep reminding myself that it's work. Just part of the job.

"Callie? I'm ready."

"Just a second!" I check the temperature of the tub and shake my hand dry as I go into Liam's bedroom.

Liam is standing shirtless with a towel wrapped around his waist, leaning on the back of his chair for support. And, my God, I don't know how he's managed to get even hotter over the past ten years. I get what it means now for a man to age like a fine wine, because *goddamn*, his body is tight and lean. He has muscles I didn't even know were muscles. Not to mention the hair across his chest and the happy trail leading down from his belly button to the place where the towel covers him.

I'm fucking wet just looking at him.

Liam clears his throat, looking down, pieces of brown hair falling over his eyes. Shit, did he notice I was staring?

"Why'd you get up? I would have helped you," I say, rushing to his side.

"I'm not an invalid. I can do some things myself."

I wrap my arm around Liam's waist as I've done many times before, but now that his skin is bare, I can feel the warmth of him... just as I did so many years ago.

It's all part of the job, Callie. All part of the job.

I have to repeat this over and over in my head as I support Liam as we make our way into the bathroom. Suddenly, his musk is a heavenly scent. Pheromones. I swallow back the feelings of arousal, but it's so hard when I'm tucked under his arm like this.

Now, to navigate getting him into the tub.

"Why don't you... drop the towel and I'll get behind you and help you in?"

Liam raises an eyebrow. "Drop the towel? You want an eyeful of something, Callie?"

With any other client, this would be sexual harassment. With Liam, I welcome it, though I'm not going to let him know it. "How else are you going to get into the tub?"

Liam looks at the tub, looks at me, then nods. "I'll crawl."

My jaw drops. "You can't be serious."

"I'm not too good to crawl, Callie."

I can't help but snicker. I back away from him. "Okay, fine."

"Turn around. No peeking. I know you have a thing for asses."

I gasp. How dare he mention something from our past? Although a small part of me loves that he remembers that I just couldn't get enough of his cute ass. I turn around and wait.

Behind me, I hear the towel fall to the ground. My mind immediately goes to thoughts of his dick. I've never seen it, at least not bare. But I saw it many times, hard through his pants. And it was impressive.

This is your job, Callie! Stop sexualizing the client!

It's impossible not to when he's such a fine specimen and I have memories of our hands running over each other's bodies and lips intertwining in the deepest, neediest kisses I've had in my life.

The water splashes and sloshes. Liam blows a raspberry. "There's soap in my mouth! Why'd you use so much bubble bath."

"To protect your dignity. Can I turn around now?"

"Yeah."

I turn to find Liam buried under all the bubbles. He looks like a little boy at bath time, just with a thick, growing beard. "Alright, let's get started."

I kneel beside the tub, retrieve the sponge, suds it up, and get to work. I'm going to take this slow. For everyone's benefit. I run the sponge over one shoulder than the other, moving it up his neck. Liam groans.

"That feels nice."

"Yeah, being clean feels nice."

"Shut up, Emerson."

I giggle and roll my sleeves up. "I don't remember you being so... stubborn."

Liam laughs, gripping onto the edge of the tub. "I have to be these days. People from all sides always trying to push me around. What I should write, who I should make deals with..."

I polish the sponge across his broad back, resisting the urge to plant a kiss at the base of his neck.

"I know what I want. I don't like when people try to get in my way."

"Hm, is that why you're trying to do everything yourself?"

Liam shakes his head. "I'm just pissed at myself."

"Why?" I move the sponge to his arm.

"For getting in a stupid accident," he says dryly.

I shake my head and take his hand in mine, twisting his arm so I can clean the underside. "That's ridiculous. You couldn't have controlled that."

"Sure, I could have. I could have not gone skiing on a black diamond in the first place."

Yikes. "Well, hindsight is always twenty-twenty, I guess."

"Yeah, I guess."

I continue to clean in silence. Suddenly, Liam grabs my wrist. My body freezes while my blood courses hot and warm.

"What's this?"

I follow his gaze down to my forearm. *Shit.* My tattoo. I've kept it hidden most of the time I've been here, which usually isn't hard. I just wear thermal long-sleeves under my scrubs. Now, though, I've gotten careless.

"It's a tattoo," I say.

Liam's amber eyes harden onto mine. "What kind of flowers are those?"

He knows the answer. He's just daring me to say it. "Daisies," I reply casually, jerking my wrist out of his hand. "Lean back for me, I want to wash your hair."

Liam follows my instructions. I wet his hair and massage his tresses with shampoo. I'm not going to think about all the times my fingers ran through his hair. I'm not going to remember the smell of his neck where his scalp meets his neck. I'm not going to -

"Daisies, huh?"

He's onto me. "Sure, why not daisies?"

"Interesting."

I continue to scrub.

"Any particular reason?"

"Is that a leading question?"

Liam glances back at me. "Yes."

I chew on the inside of my cheek. "It seems like you want to say something you're not saying."

Liam turns, the bubbles shifting around him. Even with his hair all soapy and white, he's handsome. "I gave you daisies."

"Oh, did you? I don't recall."

He smirks. "What's it mean?"

I'm not going to entertain this conversation a second longer. "You rinse out your hair and soak for a bit. I'll come back and finish you off in a few minutes."

"Is that meant to be a double entendre?"

Fuck, he's got me so flustered. I don't dignify that question with an answer and rush out of the bathroom, not even paying attention to my surroundings until I'm safely in my room, alone. I put my hands over my face and groan.

There's no way he'll believe me if I tell him the tattoo represents so much more than him. He's too egocentric for that. He probably thinks I've been hung up on him since the moment he left Indiana and while that may or may not be true, I don't want him thinking about it.

And to make matters worse, he's made me so horny. I was wet that whole damn time.

I shake my hands anxiously and start to pace back and forth. "Breathe, Callie. Just breathe. You'll get through this."

But the waves of arousal swelling in my core aren't going away. I keep getting flashes of his beautiful, half naked body, the slightly dingy smell of his hair that set my body on fire, the knowing look in his amber eyes.

He might not be Liam Kaminsky anymore, but my feelings for him haven't changed.

Not one bit.

I drop to my knees, leaning over the edge of the bed, and bury my face in the sheets. I have to get this taken care of. Just once. Then, I can put the thoughts of him to bed and be a fucking professional.

I reach into my pants, threading my fingers under my panties and touch the slickness of my pussy.

I'm wetter than wet.

And he didn't even have to do anything.

My body is all out of whack. Seeing him took me so off-guard, it doesn't know how to handle it yet. That's okay. I can train it.

For now, though, we have to get this done.

I start to finger my clitoris gently, my breath seizing at the pulse of arousal flooding through me. I get into a good groove, kneading my sensitive spot over and over.

This is just work. Not pleasure. I am just doing this to get my job done. Which means there's no need for fantasy.

This masturbation is simply business.

However, I can't stave off the thoughts of Liam. How his fingers might do the work for me. Much better than this. I think about him finding his way into my entrance, curling up inside me, pressing my most sensitive, elusive part.

I moan into the bed and widen my knees on the ground. Nothing's even happening and yet just the thought of Liam has me moaning in pleasure.

This is not good.

His thumb would press against my clit tenderly and he'd watch me. Liam's always been a watcher. Always looking for new stories in the people around him. Watching me writhe in pleasure under his hand would just be research for him. God, how I hate him.

God, how I hate I that I *want* him.

I move my fingers faster and faster and faster until the feeling inside me snaps like a rubber band and pleasure spurts through my body. I groan, latching my free hand into the sheets, gripping them so hard I'm afraid I might tear them.

Deep breaths, Callie.

I fall back onto my heels, gasping for air, unsure of what's just happened to me.

And though pleasure is still coursing through my veins, terror strikes my heart.

I have to go back into the bathroom and face him. With the daises on my arm and the knowledge I've just come to the thought of him.

I purse my lips together tightly and growl.

Liam Sterling might have gotten the best of me this time. But I'm not going to let it happen again.

Chapter 7

Liam

I scratch my fingernails through my beard. I have to shave this thing. It's easier to let it grow than to keep up with shaving, but it's starting to get itchy. I barely recognize myself in a mirror anymore.

"Liam..."

"I'm thinking." Callie and I have been up writing for several hours now. I'm not sure what time it is, and I don't care. I've got three more chapters of this book to get done in order to meet my deadline.

"But Liam–"

"Hush!" I'm not trying to be mean, but Callie has a way of poking the bear. "This will go faster if you stop interrupting me." I shut my eyes tight and try to focus on the plot.

All that comes to mind, though, is the past three weeks. Three weeks of Callie. Of recovery. Of writing.

Despite my publisher offering to push back the deadline of my latest novel, I refused. I might be physically injured, but mentally... well I underestimated the toll that this would take on my mental health. I'm tired all the time, thinking about if my hand will ever be usable to the fullest extent again, my muscles ache, I can't do for myself things I've done my whole life.

It's been hard to feel creative.

And now, I've fallen immensely behind. Just a week to go. And nearly a third of the book left.

I'm barely treading water here.

"Liam."

"Hm?" I look at Callie. She always wears her reading glasses when we're writing together. I owe her quite an acknowledgment when the book is finished.

She juts her chin forward. "What's next?"

I clear my throat. "Um. I don't know. Still thinking."

Callie sighs and checks her smartwatch. "Liam, it's late."

"It's always late." I don't usually like to start writing until it's dark.

"It's one."

"So?" With the way I work, I don't give a shit about what time I finish. I finish when I finish.

Callie looks away from me nervously. "We had a long day today."

Every day has been a long day of therapy. Today was no different.

"You should get to bed. So we can do it again tomorrow."

"I'm not done writing, Callie."

Her eyes flutter shut. "I know, but –"

"If you're tired, fine, go to bed, but I'm finishing the chapter. Okay? I've got a fucking deadline."

"Don't swear at me, Liam."

"I didn't swear at you."

"Yes, you did."

I laugh ruefully. "I swore, but I didn't swear *at* you, alright?"

Callie is silent. She takes off her glasses and polishes them on her pajama top. It's clear Callie is a full-grown woman now, but she still wears matching pajamas. Floral pants and top. It's adorable. Almost like a grandmother. A really smoking hot grandmother.

Anyway. The story. The plot. The chapter. "You know, I'll be better off doing this alone. Even with just one hand. I can hunt and peck no problem."

Callie's shoulders drop and she stares at me.

"Alright? You call it a night; I'll see you in the morning."

Her eyes narrow.

"Callie..."

"You're going to bed. Now."

"No, I'm not. And don't talk to me like I'm a–"

"You said to me you want to get better as fast as possible. The first day I was here. Remember?" she says, jaw tense.

Yeah, I guess I did say that.

"For your sake and mine, I want to follow through on that."

"For yours?"

"Yeah, so I'm not stuck here writing your books in the middle of the night." Callie scrolls through the document. *"Her eyes swam with tears. All these years, she hadn't forgotten him. Some nights, she forgot she was alone in bed, only to reach for him and remember. He was dead."* She rolls her eyes and gags. "I mean..."

"That's not bad!"

"It's not *good* either!" Callie tosses the sheet to the side.

I feel my temper rising. She can't criticize my work like that. But I also need her. "What's wrong with it?"

Callie laughs and stands. "Well, for starters, she's pathetic."

"Pathetic?"

"You've written a character obsessed with her dead husband who she still is desperately in love with. That, I can buy." Callie walks toward me. "But as a reader, I can't root for her because she's not trying to do anything to stop it."

I start to speak, but Callie holds up her finger.

"And I know what you're doing with the subplot of her secret romance with the detective and that's fun. That's great. I love that Millie gets her happy ending, but her happiness can't rely on a man loving her despite her *damage*."

I consider this for a moment. "I didn't think about that."

"Of course, you didn't. You're used to men being written with depth and without being defined by the love in their life."

I watch Callie for a moment. From the moment she arrived, that's exactly how I've been defining her. As the woman whose heart I had broken. But she's had ten long years to recover and just because there's a daisy tattoo on her arm doesn't mean it has anything to do with me. Right?

Guess even I need to be taught a lesson every now and then. "So, we have to rewrite."

"Just bits and pieces." Callie marches over to my chair. "But not tonight. I'm gonna roll you now."

I don't have the energy to refuse her. She's right. I'm exhausted. Beyond exhausted. But once I'm in bed every night, my mind is reeling with what comes next.

In the bedroom, Callie parks me near the bed and starts to help me out. I wave her off. "I got it."

"Liam–"

"Just listen to me for a second."

She perches her hands on her hips. "As if I'm not listening to you all the time."

I ignore that comment. With all the strength left in me for the day, I push myself up out of the chair. My bum hand won't grip the arm, but my palm does the trick. Callie turns down the bed covers. I take a seat on the edge of the bed and sigh.

"You're tired, aren't you?" she asks in a soft voice. Almost reminds me of my mother.

I chuckle. "I'm not giving you that satisfaction."

"Fine." Callie steps back and crosses her arms.

My bed is high off the ground and though I've gained much of my strength back, my exhaustion is weighing heavy on me. "Would you mind... my legs..." I start to move them slightly.

She smiles. "Not at all."

Callie helps guide my legs up onto bed and, as she does so, I start to lay back on the pillows, letting out a long, contented sigh.

"Feels good, doesn't it?" she asks, pulling the covers over me.

As I stare up at her, I can't help but wish she was spending the night with me. Crawling under the covers to me, swirling her body around mine. "Could you give me another pillow?"

Callie sighs. It never seems like exasperation, though. "Sure." She grabs a pillow from the other side of the bed and starts to fluff it up.

"You're way too nice to me," I say raggedly.

"Yes, I am. But my bank account has never looked better. Up."

I push myself up and allow her to tuck the pillow behind me. Up close, I can smell her freshly washed blonde hair, mostly dry now. I can see her nipples poking through her night shirt. It's like she wants me to notice how beautiful she's grown.

"There. Now, sire, is there anything else you might need?" Callie asks in a melodramatic accent.

Before she can step away from the bed, I stop her. "Wait."

Callie frowns.

"I have a question."

"Okay..."

"Have you told Nate that you're here?" Three weeks and I haven't dared bring him up.

Callie sinks down to the edge of the bed and shakes her head. "No."

A crack splits my heart. "Why?"

"Do you want him to know that I'm here?"

"He doesn't know anything happened between us, does he?"

She stops breathing.

"You never told him, did you?"

"Why would I have done that?"

"I don't know. Guilt or shame or–"

"Liam, our relationship might have been a lot of things, but I've never felt ashamed of it. Have you?"

My eyes widen. "No, no of course not."

"Really?"

I reach out and touch her arm. Don't care if I should or shouldn't. I need her to hear me. "Really. I promise."

Callie's head droops like that of a dying flower. "Then why'd you... why'd you leave?"

"Because we couldn't. You know we couldn't."

"Why not?"

I pull her arm closer to me. I don't want her to run away as she's been known to do since moving in here with me. "Because there was just no way we could have made it work."

"Maybe you couldn't have. But I could have." Her blue eyes glimmer with determination. I don't doubt what she's said for a second.

I nod. "You're stronger than me. I've known that since I met you."

Callie laughs wryly. "That's not true."

With my last bit of strength, I sit up. I'm close to her for the first time without reason other than I want to be. "It is. I was weak. A coward. It's why I couldn't stop myself from..." I swallow. Her lips are right there. Ruby and plump and all woman. I lean in only an inch.

Callie's hand lands against my chest. I raise my eyes to hers. Sadness in her eyes. Chest tight with self-restraint. "Don't."

It's like she can read my mind. We knew each other ten years ago for a month, and somehow, we've always been umbilically connected. How could she tell how much I wanted to kiss her?

Why did she say no?

Callie unwinds herself from my arms, gets up, and goes to the door. "Goodnight, Liam," she murmurs. Then, she turns off the light and closes the door behind her.

I collapse back onto the bed, staring at the ceiling. I was exhausted only a minute ago. Now I'm wide awake, remembering the moment Callie ruined my life.

⋘◆⋙

Ten years earlier...

"Hello!" Nate's mother shouts from the top step. She looks just like him, save the graying hair and her pudgy middle.

I sling my rucksack over my shoulder, my whole life for the next month stuffed inside. I let Nate run ahead to greet his mother. Must be nice to return to the place he's called home his whole life.

I just feel like I'm always looking for the next thing.

"Ma, this is Liam."

"Liam! Come here!" Mrs. Emerson pulls me into a hug just as tight as the one she gave Nate. "Nate's told us so much about you!"

When she releases me, she sighs. "I'm sorry my husband isn't here to greet you. He'll be home around dinner."

"Where's Cal?" Nate asks.

Mrs. Emerson huffs. "Well, she said she'd be right down when I told her I'd spotted your car. Let's see. Callie! Calllllie!"

"Coming!" We hear Callie call from inside the house.

"I'm sorry, Callie's a little scatter-brained. Enjoying her last summer before she's off to college. Can you believe it?"

Nate groans. "Don't remind me."

"That's exciting," I say, unsure what more to offer.

The front door swings open and I lose all cogent thought when my eyes land on the girl I assume to be Callie Emerson. I see a mop of blonde hair on her head, freckles across her nose, beaming blue eyes...and barely any clothes on. She's clad in just a bikini top and shorts.

This is not the girl I'd seen in Nate's pictures of his little sister, eight years younger than him. I imagined I'd be meeting the girl who still had braces and hadn't hit puberty.

But Callie Emerson isn't a girl. She's a woman.

"Natey!"

"Cal!"

The two of them tear into a hug. He swings her around and then drops her right in front of me. "Callie, this is Liam."

And when our eyes lock and her pretty lips part, I know I'm totally done for.

Chapter 8

Callie

*P**resent day...*
"You know, for such an expensive place, there's not a lot to do here," I grumble and then take a big snapping bite of a celery stick.

Wade laughs. He's got a soaring kind of giggle that dances like water. "Once you get past all the leather and mahogany, it's sort of just a house, isn't it?"

"Are you talking about the penthouse or a sex dungeon?" Emma asks jokingly from behind the refrigerator door where she's making notes of what groceries need to be purchased.

I spend a lot of time in the kitchen with Wade or in the laundry room with Emma. They're good friends themselves and have quickly brought me into their fold. They don't have even a whiff of the history between Liam and me. I'm eager to keep it that way.

"You ought to take a day and get the hell out. Why are you always here?" Wade asks, handing me a julienned piece of jicama.

I shrug. "I don't know. All my friends are nurses and doctors, and their shift schedules are insane. It's hard to catch them." I've talked with Sasha on the phone several times, never for more than ten minutes. Her residency has been kicking her ass. "Plus, everyone's in Brooklyn. It's like being in a long-distance relationship."

"Mm. True. You know, I once dated a guy on Long Island while I was still living at home with my folks in the Bronx. Insanity," Emma replies.

Wade shakes his head. "Still, you can't spend your days cooped up in here like J.D. Salinger. You need to get out. You're young, just cause you're working here doesn't mean you don't have a life."

The way they're talking to me makes it sound like I'm a complete hermit. That's not the total truth. But between how isolated I am here on the Upper East Side, the prices, and the how goddamn cold it's been, it's been hard to get out.

"What's it feel like out there today? Cold?"

"Not bad."

"But that comes from a native New Yorker," Emma chides Wade.

I munch on the stick of jicama. Fresh air does a body good. Could do Liam wonders. The most time he's spent outside is on the terrace. The wind is so vicious out there though he's barely out there for three minutes before he demands to come back inside. "I've got an idea."

<hr />

"Really, Callie– "

"You'll be fine." I tighten the scarf around Liam's neck, not stopping until he chokes. "Sorry."

Liam adjusts the wool scarf and glares. "It's cold out."

"It's not bad out. No windchill."

Liam shakes his head. "Well, it's a Wednesday."

"And?"

"And it's busy out there on Wednesdays."

I laugh and push him through the door of the apartment. "It's New York. It's busy every day!"

Liam grumbles something to himself.

"You want to press the elevator button?" I ask in an infantilizing tone.

Liam glares even harder. "Do you mind, Mother?"

"Not at all." I press the button for him. The elevator groans and we wait.

"Really, Callie, this is... silly."

"No one has ever called a walk through Central Park silly."

The elevator doors open and I roll Liam inside. "Well, I am. I think it's silly."

"I think you're scared."

"I'm not fucking scared," he spits through his beard. He had enough where-withal to give it a trim the other day. Now it sits on his face nicely, showing off his chiseled jaw and cheekbones. His hair is still growing down past his ears. He looks like a mountain man rather than a metropolitan author.

"Okay, then indulge me. One little stroll around the park."

The doors ding open and immediately Frederick spots us. "Oh! Mr. Sterling! Ms. Emerson!"

"Jesus Christ," Liam mutters to himself, pinching his nose bridge.

"Hello, Frederick!" I greet him chipperly.

"Mr. Sterling, you're looking quite well. I haven't seen you in weeks."

Liam forces a smile. "As was intended and planned until–"

"We're just getting some fresh air. A little spin around the park."

Frederick walks by my side as I roll Liam's chair through the lobby. "A perfect day for a walk. Very warm. Balmy even. Ha!"

I grin even though it's clear Liam can't stand Frederick's friendliness. He's such a grump. It seems as if nothing brings him much happiness these days.

The front doors slide open, and a burst of cold air hits us. Balmy is not how I would describe it. Liam flinches, his eyes squinting at the midday sun. I hear him curse under his breath.

"Alright, be safe out there. As always call me if you need anything. Even a rescue mission!" Frederick announces.

I laugh. "Will do!"

As soon as we are a bit down the block and out of ear shot, Liam growls, "That guy drives me nuts."

"Why? He's so nice."

"Exactly. Always so nice. Always so happy. And you can tell it's just innate. No medication would bring me that level of joy."

I shrug. "Well, if you can't beat 'em, join 'em."

We arrive at the crosswalk, and I immediately notice Liam's body tensing. "You alright?"

"Just everything's moving so fast."

Of course, it is. He's been cooped up in that penthouse for a month straight. Before that, he was recovering in the hospital. And before that... sliding down ski slopes without a care in the world. Or so, I assume. This must be kind of a shock for him.

A car speeds through the intersection, horn blaring. Liam jerks back. I put a hand on his shoulder. "It's fine. Just a car. We're okay." The signal changes from stop to walk. "You good?"

Liam's good hand reaches back and covers mine. He holds on tight and nods. "Y-yeah."

I don't mind the feeling of his gloved hand holding tight to mine. In fact, I like it. It makes me feel like he needs me. Sure, I've been helping him get stronger and taking care of his needs for the past month, but I always feel slight disdain from him. It is always mired in his shame of not being able to take care of himself.

For just a split second, I'm needed and wanted.

That's a powerful feeling.

Shake it off. Just the job.

We cross the street and into the park. Liam lets go of my hand then and I let myself feel disappointed for a split second.

But just a second.

Central Park is just as magical as everyone makes it out to be with all the winding paths and landmarks. You could get lost here and never want to leave. I take a left and we wander through the leafless trees and gray grass. Even in winter, it's beautiful.

The paved path, luckily, isn't too bumpy for Liam's chair. And the park isn't too busy. We get kind smiles from strangers. I smile back while Liam avoids eye contact.

"This is nice, isn't it?"

"It's... fine."

That's Liam's current code for good. I'll take it.

We wind down the path to a reservoir of water that's frozen over. The ice is ungroomed, but that hasn't stopped people from breaking out their skates and gliding around.

"People usually use this for launching model boats," Liam says.

"Oh, model boats. How very... elite," I say with melodramatic flair.

Liam laughs. "You make people on the Upper East Side sound like characters on *Monty Python*."

"Well, they are. A little. You wanna stop for a while?"

I push Liam to a bench overlooking the frozen pond. On the ice, a father and a small child are playing a very relaxed game of ice hockey while an older woman skates around with the utmost grace. I sit on the end of the bench so I'm next to Liam and look out at the pond.

It's almost romantic, if I don't think about the reality of the situation.

Out of nowhere, Liam says, "You're right. This is nice."

I half expect him to then add that he's ready to go home, but he doesn't. "I'm glad you think so."

"Yeah. Almost glad you made me come out here," he says with a lopsided smile.

Oo, that smile. That's the smile that got me into trouble the first time. *Don't look too closely, Callie. Don't want to fall and break your heart again.* I reach into my bag and pull out a thermos. "You want some hot chocolate? Wade made it for me."

Liam half-laughs, expecting me to be joking, but then sees the thermos. "Um. Sure. I haven't had hot chocolate in years."

I crack open the thermos and pour some hot chocolate (or *chocolat chaud*, as Wade called it) into the cup. "I hope you don't mind if we share."

"You have cooties?" Liam teases.

"Lots of them."

"Good. Then you do the honors."

I take a sip of the warm, brown liquid. So rich and creamy. Swiss Miss could never. "Mmm. Delicious."

I hand the cup over to Liam and he takes it excitedly. "Wade is a marvel." Then he sips it. I can see the warmth travel through his body. His shoulders relax, and he sighs, at peace. At least for a second. "I have to say Callie, I was hoping if I ever saw you again, I'd be in better shape than this."

I glance at Liam, taken aback. "I didn't think you'd ever thought about me after you left."

He snorts. "Oh, come on. I might have been the one to leave, but that doesn't mean I just forgot about you." His eyes soften.

Amber honey. I shiver.

"How could I have?" he continues.

I turn away and focus on the skaters dancing across the ice. "Well, it's been a long time. And you might have been my first love, but I know I wasn't yours."

"Well, not every woman is my best friend's little sister. And very few I've lived with in a house for a month."

I laugh. "I was... so childish."

"No. Not childish. Young. You were young." Liam sips some more hot chocolate and hands the cup back over to me. "So was I, I guess. Maybe not in age, but in the way you made me feel."

"Is that why you kissed me in the hall? Trying to sneak something out of my fountain of youth."

"No, nothing like that." Liam leans his head back and looks at me. "It was just because I wanted to kiss you. I'd forgotten what it meant to be full of hope and optimism. And there you were, bubbling over with it." He turns and stares out at the pond. "It was intoxicating."

Intoxication is not a way I thought he would describe our relationship. If anything, I was fawning over him, and he was indulging me. Not... intoxicated by me.

"You're the reason I'm here today, you know."

"What?"

"Why I'm a writer. Why I have the life I have." He takes a deep breath. "You inspired me to go after what I really wanted."

"That's ridiculous."

"it's not, it's the truth."

"If it was the truth then why wouldn't you have wanted more? You know?"

Liam rubs his chin, hair scratching through his fingers. "Callie, if we had stayed together, it would have been a disaster. You would have felt used up by me. Trust me. I'm sure that's how Nate feels."

"What do you mean?"

"Everyone in my life has had to suffer because I sacrificed so much to get where I am. Time, energy, attention. It all went to my work so I could get off the godforsaken rig. Nate might have been born for that kind of life, but not me. Not me at all."

I smile softly. "You don't have to let me down easy again, Liam. I'm over it."

"Well, that's good." He gazes at me and smiles. "One of us has to be."

I have to keep from gasping. He's not over it? Over us? Does he have regrets? Or does he think we met at the wrong time?

Regardless, I don't say anything more about it. But I do reach across his lap, take his bad hand in mine, and wrap his fingers around my hand.

Neither of us speaks.

But the electricity sparking between our hands says a whole lot.

Chapter 9

Liam

For the first time in weeks, I'm sitting in front of the laptop. Not to write, but to motivate myself. I've been doing the hand exercises that Callie has instructed me to do, staring at the thing I desperately want to be able to do again, hoping somehow the woo-woo Gen Z trick of manifesting will translate to me.

Wrist extension and flexion off the edge of the table, supination and pronation, radial deviation. All these technical words that I've committed to memory in further hopes that understanding will somehow solve my problem.

"Mr. Sterling?"

I look up to find Emma peeking her head out from the hallway.

"Are you alright?"

"Yes. Why?"

"I just have never seen you do your exercises on your own."

I look at my hand and then try to clench it in a fist before dropping it into my lap. "Well, better late than never, I guess."

She smiles sweetly, although Emma's smile always has a hint of mischief. "Callie will be very happy to hear that when she comes back."

"Yes, did she say when she'd be back, by the way? It's getting late." For the first time since Callie has been working for me, she's taken a jaunt back to Brooklyn to see a friend. Sara? Tosha? Can't quite remember the girl's name.

It's her right, obviously, to have time off and take care of her own life.

But, as strange as it is to admit it, I miss her.

"I don't know. Why? Do you miss her?" Emma asks in a teasing voice.

I pick up a pen with my good hand and lob it across the room at her. She dodges it, returning to where she came from with a tittering laugh. I'm quite positive that Wade and Emma know nothing of my history with Callie. However, I guess it's hard to ignore that we've become closer. Instead of moving around the apartment like poles of magnets that can never touch, things have softened between us. More moments of... friendship, I guess.

I'll admit that I've perhaps pushed a flirtation here and there. I can't help it. She brings it out of me. Plus, revisiting our past, even if we're too afraid to speak the details, brings me a level of nostalgia I haven't felt in quite some time. Since becoming *Liam Sterling*, I'm always looking ahead, rarely behind.

It's refreshing.

A buzzing sound interrupts my reverie. My phone vibrating is on the table. I pick it up. My heart drops when I see the caller.

Nate Emerson.

Since I left the rig, Nate and I are in a perpetual state of phone tag. However, he hasn't reached out since Callie's started here and I certainly haven't either, too afraid that I might accidentally say something too revealing.

Without Callie in the penthouse, though, I think I can play it cool.

"Hello?" I answer gruffly.

"Well, well, well..."

"Hi, Nate."

"Can't believe I caught you."

"Yeah, you called at a good time."

Nate chuckles. "You know, if I didn't know better, I'd say I think you've been avoiding me."

I swallow.

"I know you're exorbitantly busy though with all the *writing*."

I keep my identity pretty well protected. Even my photo on every book jacket has my face obscured. But Nate was my best friend during the time in my life I was putting this all together. He had to be party to it. And, given Callie's surprise, I think he's done a damn good job of keeping my pen name under wraps.

"So, how've you been?"

"Well, I've been better."

"What's up?"

"I... uh... got in a skiing accident."

Nate gasps. "Holy shit, man! Are you okay?"

I laugh. "I mean, I'm alive."

"You know what I mean."

"Yeah, I know. I'm in a chair for now. I was paralyzed from the waist down for a few days. It went away, but it's left my legs really weak." I squeeze my bad hand as best I can. "And my hand... hasn't been the same since."

Nate sighs sympathetically. "I'm so sorry. I'm glad it's not worse, but–"

"Yeah, could have been better. Could have been way worse." I haven't really thought of it like that until now. I could have been permanently paralyzed, could have been confined to a chair the rest of my life. With Callie around, I have been able to make strides (no pun intended) toward normalcy. I've been so caught up in what I've been missing that I haven't really processed how horrible it could have been. "I'm just cooped up here in this penthouse."

"A prison of luxury."

I laugh. "Exactly."

"I ought to send Callie to you."

My stomach bottoms out. I for sure think my intestines are littering the ground. "Oh?"

"Yeah, she's–didn't I tell you this?"

Shit, did he tell me this? Am I really that bad of a listener? A bad friend?

"She's now a personal nurse. Live-in and all that. No longer at the hospital. She just started her new assignment otherwise, I'd send her your way. I'm sure you guys would have a lot of catching up to do."

Oh my God, when will this end? "I'm sure. It's been, what? Ten years?"

"Wow. Time really flies." I can hear Nate smiling and suddenly get a flash of deja vu of all the times in the bunks when we would be shooting the shit when we should have been sleeping.

I lick my upper lip. "So, how is Callie?"

"She's great."

"I guess she's all grown up now, huh?"

Nate guffaws. "Yeah, don't remind me. I still see my little sister, braces and all. Watching her date causes me an unreasonable amount of rage, especially given the jackasses she's chosen."

So, Nate's still as protective of his little sister as he was back in the day. Noted. I would hate to be on the receiving end of that rage. After all, that's part of the reason I called things off back in the day. Nate had confided in me how scared he was for Callie to go to school that fall. "She's so innocent. So sweet. I'd hate for her to lose that because guys can be such idiots. You know what I mean, right?"

I don't think Nate ever suspected anything was happening, but I couldn't help but think that was his subtle way of telling me to back off.

Not that I would ever act on what's happening between Callie and me *now*. Never. Besides, nothing's happening.

Right?

"But I'm proud of her. She's worked so hard to get where she is now."

"I bet."

"And she's her own person. I can't be too–"

The sound of Nate' voice is interrupted by a beeping on my phone. I pull it back and see on the screen there's an incoming call from my publisher. *Shit.* "Uh, Nate, I hate to cut this short, but my publisher is on the other line and –"

"Don't sweat it man. Take care of yourself, alright?"

My stomach twists. I didn't even ask Nate about his life. How the job is going, about his wife and girls, if he still loves the sea air as much as he did back in the day.

Damn, I'm a shit friend... on top of going behind his back with his sister.

I can't think about that now, though. Because Ron, my publisher is on the other line. "Ron! How are you?"

"I've been better." His tone is coarse.

"Uh, alright."

"Do you know what day it is?"

Oh, I know what day it is. The due date of my manuscript. I've kept a detailed countdown. I just have a couple chapters left. A full week of work. But I couldn't bring myself to tell Ron. I didn't want to show my cards that I'm floundering after I was adamant there needed to be no changes made to my schedule. "Friday?"

"Hardee har har," Ron says dryly.

I hear the front door open and look in the direction of the hall. Emma and Callie greet each other excitedly. More distractions. "Listen, Ron–"

"Don't 'listen, Ron' me! I told you we'd push back the deadline, didn't I?"

I swallow. "You did."

"And now here we are. Nighttime. I don't have a manuscript."

I try to smile. "It's not even midnight. You know, I'm always a bit of a night owl."

Callie waltzes into the room, about to greet me, but stops when she realizes I'm on the phone. She smiles and waves silently. God, she's so cute. I'd much rather be talking to her right now instead of stodgy Ron.

"Can I expect the manuscript before midnight, Liam?"

I clear my throat. "I've got three chapters left. If I double time, I can get it to you by–"

"You're kidding, right?"

"No."

"You're lucky you're our biggest seller, Liam. Otherwise–"

Callie looks at me with concern. I look away, closing my eyes. "I know. I know. I'm lucky. I'm sorry."

"We're willing to work around your injuries, Liam. It's not a problem. But you need to communicate what you need."

"Well, I just need a few days. That's all."

Callie starts to come toward me, tentative, like she's approaching a lone wolf.

"You're lucky you're *you*. Any other writer would be on thin ice."

"Yeah. Got it."

"I want the manuscript by Monday."

"Monday. Alright." I purse my lips and sigh. "Thanks."

Ron hangs up without another word. I drop the phone on the table and bury my face in my hands, my bum hand curling with stiffness. "Shit, shit, shit."

"What's wrong?" Callie asks softly.

"I'm late. The manuscript was supposed to be in by tonight and I couldn't finish it and–"

"I would have stayed to help if I had known–"

"No! Stop. You deserved a day off, I'm not gonna..." I sigh heavily. "I thought I could do it. But my hand is..."

Callie crouches beside my chair, takes my decrepit hand in hers, and looks up at me, concern lacing her brow together. "What can I do to help now?"

I shake my head. "You don't have to do anything."

"I don't have to. But I want to."

I swallow as I look into her sparkling blue eyes. Her cheeks are blushed. Not from winter wind, but from libations that I can smell on her breath. She's not drunk, just tipsy. But I've most certainly ruined her high.

"We can do it. I know we can. We've got until Monday, right?" Callie releases my hand, leaving an emptiness in my heart. She sits in the chair nearest mine and spins the laptop toward her, curling her fingers over the keyboard, ready to go. "No better time to start than right now, hm?"

From the moment Callie arrived, she's been willing to help me. Sure, sometimes it involved a little pulling of teeth, but she's provided ministry to me when I've been at my worst. I don't think I deserve that.

So why the hell do I think I deserve a second chance?

"Liam?"

I scratch the side of my head, curls of overgrown hair swirling through my fingers. "Alright. Let's do it.

Callie grins at me. "Wade!"

Wade comes in, his coat half on. "Yes?"

"Can you put a pot of coffee on before you go?"

He cracks a smile. "You got it, Cal."

"Oh, and Wade?"

"Yes."

I can't help but be endeared to Callie's tipsiness. She only got drunk once all those years ago when I bought us a pack of beer and we drank it while sitting in the trunk of her car in a cornfield. She'd never gotten drunk before, but three Miller Lites did the trick. I drove her home and had to sneak her into her room without her family hearing me come up the stairs.

"Can you put out some of your homemade pretzels to defrost? We're gonna need some snacks."

Wade laughs. "I'm already on it."

"You're the best."

Wade disappears back into the kitchen.

Callie cracks her fingers and looks at me with a determined smirk. "Alright. What comes next?"

If it wasn't apparent before, it's abundantly clear now. This girl is a fucking drug, and I cannot get enough of her.

Chapter 10

Callie

"There's a possibility we can move some people around and get you started with a new client in a couple weeks. Does that interest you?"

I stare out the big windows facing Fifth Avenue and try to process this information. "Um..."

"You said you weren't too happy with your client at the outset. Has that changed?" Polly asks.

I glance back at the parallel bars that are still idling from our interrupted session. Liam received a call from his publisher he had to take, so he rolled straight into the library for privacy. I took this as a good moment to make a phone call of my own. I was planning on letting Polly know she wouldn't have to continue looking for a new placement for me as things had gotten better here, but she greeted me with this information instead. "You know, it just took some time to settle in. Things have definitely been better, but... if it makes more sense for me to go somewhere else..."

"If it's working, let's not ruin a good thing," Polly cuts me off. "I'm glad to hear that it's gone better than you expected it to."

Outside, snowflakes are pouring down from the sky. We're expecting a huge blizzard. Liam told Emma and Wade to stay home, that the two of us would be okay alone for the day.

I'm not sure if that's how I would describe it.

After working nonstop over the weekend on the manuscript, Liam and I have become closer than ever. Just being close to him and having him trust me with his work fills me with pride and a desire to be *even closer*. I've gotten better at typing, too. My words per minute has increased significantly. I could be a *great* assistant should I ever be looking for a career change.

When we finished, it was late on Sunday night. My fingers were tired, the muscles having never been worked so hard. And the two of us celebrated with silence and awe. Liam reached out to me and touched the small of my neck. "Thank you," he whispered.

And for a split second, I thought he might kiss me.

Every moment since, I've felt he might kiss me.

I wouldn't dare be the one to cross that line first. But if he did?

I wouldn't say no.

"Can I help you with anything else, Callie?" Polly asks.

"N-no. Thank you."

"Of course. Stay safe today. Hope you don't have any errands to run."

I shake my head. "We're hunkered down."

"Good. Take care."

Polly hangs up expediently. I drop my phone into the pocket of my scrubs and look out at the snow, crossing my arms.

The two of us are alone in the penthouse. We've had nights upon nights like this. But always, during the day, at least one of Emma or Wade is here.

Now, just us.

And it thrills me in a terrifying sort of way.

I'll have to keep a schedule. Finish up the rehab session, make him some lunch, have him take a nap, maybe rest myself. Keep busy. That's the only way we're not going to fall into–

"He loves it."

I turn and find Liam emerging from the hallway to the library. Except he's not in his chair. He has one hand on the wall just in case he needs the help, but he's... walking. "What are you doing?"

"Says it's my best work." He's beaming. I haven't seen him so happy since my arrival.

"Why aren't you in your chair?" My eyes are welling with tears. He's walking with strength and vigor, probably using everything he has in him to make sure he can balance.

Liam grins. "Don't need it."

He's coming closer to me, each step a labor of strength.

"I couldn't have done it without you," he says.

Instinctually, I back away from him, step by step until I feel the cold pane of the window hit my back. It's not that I'm afraid of him.

I'm afraid of what he has in him.

"I couldn't write without you. Couldn't finish the story without you."

"You could have. I promise. You could have."

Liam shakes his head, only a foot away now. I've forgotten how tall he is. Well over six feet, pure muscle and dominance. I feel tiny. Like a little girl. Like I did ten years ago. In his chair, he shrinks. No wonder he's lost so much of his confidence by being forced to recover. "How can I thank you?"

"By getting back in your chair, Liam. This is dangerous..." I reply.

He laughs. "You've always been funny."

Liam takes a step closer. I hold my breath.

"Is this alright?" he asks. His voice is lolling with softness.

I should say no. I work for him. He's hurt me once before. There's no good reason for me to let him be close to me, other than I want him. I want him so bad. "Yes."

Liam reaches out and tucks a lock of hair that's fallen from my claw clip behind my ear. His wide palm settles on my cheek. "Thank you," he says, as if those two words are the most important in the English language. His amber eyes lock into mine.

I'm immediately transported into a memory. The two of us trapped in the hallway of my family's home leaning up against the wall opposite the door, waiting for Nate to come out of the shower. I was listening to his breath and wanting to put my head against his strong chest. I remember how he turned his face toward mine and looked down at me with a crinkling smile.

"Callie?" he had said as if there was an implicit question.

"Yes?"

"I don't want to scare you... but I really wanna kiss you."

It was barely eight in the morning, and I wasn't even showered. I was still crusted with sleep and smelled. And he wanted to kiss me.

And no one had ever wanted to kiss me before. Let alone tell me.

So, I let him.

Now, here I am, and I feel that same feeling brewing between us. The want to kiss.

But now we're grown and now we've both faced the world, both been broken by it in different ways.

I don't *want* to kiss him. I need to.

"Thank you," Liam repeats, lowering his face toward mine at a frustratingly sluggish pace. Almost daring me to avoid his lips.

But I won't.

"You're welcome," I whisper.

"Thank you... so much."

"You're welcome... so much." And those final two words are said right into his mouth before he kisses me.

When our lips touch, I'm afraid I might collapse to the ground. I touch his waist, pull him into me, letting warmth and arousal bloom through my body.

Liam's hand slinks from my cheek into my hair, working his lips against mine with passion. I slide one hand around him to his back, gripping at the fabric of his shirt.

Liam moans into my mouth. If we're honest with ourselves, these past five weeks have all been adding up to this.

"Callie..." he whispers, nose nudging my cheek.

"Yes, Liam?" I reply.

"My biggest regret..."

I close my eyes.

"...is that I wasn't your first."

I push my forehead against his, our lips brushing together. It's my biggest regret, too. Instead of Liam, a man I was falling in love with, I lost my virginity the first week of college at a frat party to a sophomore with acne who said he had a reputation for making girls' first times good.

I would have much rather had my first time with someone I trusted with my whole being, who I knew would take care of me.

"And I know I can never be that, but can I... will you let me..." Each phrase is punctuated with an effortful, heavy breath. Both from exertion and also from the way his cock is laboring against my belly. Liam swallows hard. "Let me make love to you."

I don't waste a single moment. "Yes, please," I say breathlessly, before pulling him into another kiss, our deepest one yet.

Liam's hands travel to my lower back. He squeezes me hard as if he needs to hold on tight, so I'll never disappear. Our tongues begin to duel for dominance, causing my insides to melt with pleasure. I want him deeper than ever before. I want all of him.

Liam tries to take a step back, pulling me with him, but he falters. The kiss breaks, his knees give out, and he gasps.

I might be smaller than him, but I've done this work for a long time and my strength proves enough to be able to keep him from falling to the ground like a ragdoll. I cling to him, pulling his mouth into mine once more, kissing as if it's the elixir of life.

This isn't how it would have gone all those years ago. I would not have been the one in charge. Liam would have prepared me. He would have been gentle and, though it probably would have hurt regardless, he would have taken care of me.

Now, I'm the one taking care of him. I'm the stronger one. I am the one who can lead. So, I will. "Let me get your chair."

"No, I can make it to the bed. I can make it that far."

I stare down into Liam's face, exerting every last bit of my strength to keep him from falling.

He nods adamantly. "I can, I promise I can." Desperation creeps into his voice. He wants to prove himself to me. He can't sacrifice his pride, even when we're both so vulnerable. Liam pushes himself back up to standing with a grunt and shakes his hair back out of his face.

"Let me help you," I murmur.

"Callie–" he begins to refuse, but as soon as my hand touches his, he goes silent.

I pull his arm over my shoulder and wrap my arms around his ribs. "Let me."

Liam hesitates and then nods. "Okay."

Though the passion was interrupted, the walk to the bedroom vibrates with anticipation. Neither of us speaks, focusing on making sure Liam is steady and strong. But my heart pumps harder and harder as we go down the hallway to his room, then through the door, then sit him on the edge of the bed.

Liam takes measured breaths as he runs his hands up and down my sides. His hands slide under my top and together, we pull it over my head, leaving me in just my thermal and scrub bottoms. He pushes up the hem of my undershirt and trails kisses up from my belly to my sternum, all the way up to my clavicle. My head tips back in pleasure and I throw the shirt off, leaving me in just a bra.

"Goddamn, Callie, you're wearing too many layers."

I giggle. "Sorry, I didn't know this was on the schedule for today."

Liam smirks.

"I think it's your turn, actually."

"Oh, yeah?"

"Mhm..." I pull his shirt up over his head, revealing his toned chest. "Oo..." I run my hands over all his muscles and hum in pleasure.

Liam chuckles. "Like what you see?"

I kiss his shoulder. "Love."

"Come here," Liam murmurs, wrapping his arm around me and pulling me into a kiss.

We fall into the bed on our sides, lips caressing, hands exploring. Liam wraps a hand around my ass, pushing my hips to his so I can feel how hard he is, how big he is.

"I want to make you feel good."

"You already are. "

"But…" Liam reaches around me and unclips my bra "I want to make you feel really good."

To match him, I slide my hand into the waistband of his sweatpants and grab onto his length. Liam lets out a laugh of surprise, head dipping back. "Fuck…"

"I want this inside me."

"You don't have to tell me twice."

In a flurry that is as awkward as it is passionate, we remove the rest of our clothing and Liam rolls himself onto me, holding himself up on his elbows. His cock labors against my thigh, eager to be inside. His breath is audible.

"Liam, don't overextend yourself. Let me–"

"No," he says firmly. His eyes fall to my bare breasts. He plants kisses against the insides of them and then drags his lips back up my chest, to my neck, up to my ear. "*I'm* making love to *you*."

My whole body quivers. I don't have the strength to be his nurse anymore. I am at the mercy of his body.

And God how I want him.

Liam touches my hip bone and pushes the head of his cock into my opening. My body jerks and he stops. "You alright?"

"Yes, yeah, just…" I wrap my hand around the nape of his neck and lock my eyes in his. I've waited ten years for this. I want it to be good. I want it to count. "Go slow to start, alright?"

A smile cracks across his lips. "Of course."

He kisses me softly and as his tongue rolls through my mouth he pushes himself deeper inside me. Slow and steady, just as he'd promised. I moan into his mouth at the feeling of his cock stretching me.

It feels better than I ever could have imagined it would feel having Liam inside me. No doubt the anticipation has grown over the past month, built on the bones of a relationship I've wished for years to return to. But with each small pulse, I feel my body electrify. A pool of heat is starting to spread out from my pelvis.

I wrap my legs around his waist and start to pump my hips against his. Faster. Taking him deeper.

Liam groans and grits his teeth. "Fuck, you're tight."

"You feel so good," I murmur.

Liam cups my chin in his hand and dips his thumb between his lips. I wrap my lips around it, sucking on it as I would his cock. His pupils dilate so wide his eyes are almost completely black. "Holy shit, Callie, you're amazing," he says with as much of a smile as he can muster given all the exertion.

I push myself onto my elbows, kissing him fiercely. "You okay?" I ask, trying not to whimper.

"Better than okay."

"I don't want you to hurt—"

"For fuck's sake, Callie." Liam grabs my wrists and pushes me down into the pillows. "Stop worrying about me and let me fuck you."

I gasp at his strength and force. I'll let him do anything he wants with that kind of attitude.

Liam holds me down and thrusts furiously. My tits bounce with every jerk of his hips. I realize I'm shaking, from the tips of my toes up to my shoulders. The impending ecstasy is growing stronger and stronger by the moment, and I feel... holy fuck, I feel...

"My God, you're beautiful."

I feel like I'm going to come. But I feel so good I can't find the words for it. I let out a long whine.

"You feel good, baby."

I nod desperately.

"You want to come for me?"

I moan in affirmation, struggling against his grip. Liam lets me go. I immediately throw my arms around him and pull his chest flush with mine. "I want you to be close when I come."

Liam laughs low, but I can tell pleasure is creeping up on him too. "Look into my eyes, Callie. Let me see you."

Our gazes lock together just as tightly as the pressing of our hips. His intoxicating eyes are full of amber flecks that I wouldn't be able to see if I wasn't this close to him.

"Come for me, Callie."

I cling to him, running my hands through his hair. Higher and higher he brings me with every pulse of his hips.

"Please, come for me."

The need in his voice is all it takes to send me over the edge. "I'm– I'm–"

He thrusts harder and growls into my neck.

My whole body alights, bursting with fire in every nerve. I let out a long, loud moan, holding onto him as if by letting go I'd fall off the edge of a cliff. My center clenches around him, begging him to join me in this pleasure.

Liam thrusts several more times before gasping wretchedly and spilling inside me.

Thank God I'm on the pill or else this could get messy.

"Oh my God," he says on a heaving exhale. "Damn..." He rolls off of me, collapsing onto the pillow beside me.

For a while, only our breathing can be heard. Both of us trying to steady ourselves and get back to neutral.

I glance over at him, his naked form next to me in bed. I can't help but smile.

I've been waiting ten years for this.

Chapter 11

Liam

I've been waiting ten years for that.

Of course, I'd never say that out loud. But I've never forgotten about her. I've always regretted not being her first.

However, it definitely wouldn't have been as good as this was. Callie's got some skills. Just the way she had her hands wrapped in my hair made me crazy. Now, just hearing her come down, how her breath is settling again in her chest.

It gives me goosebumps.

Makes me want to do it all over again.

"Um. Wow," she says softly.

I laugh. "Yeah, wow."

I look askance to her, our eyes meeting. I feel bashful almost immediately, but I know I can't look away.

Suddenly, both of us are laughing. This is ridiculous. How did this happen? Well, I mean, I know it happened. But *how* did we get here? Really...? "Come here," I mutter, pulling her onto my chest, letting her tuck her head into my neck.

We used to do this a lot. Just lay together. That's all we really could do. Kissing and cuddling. Callie hadn't ever had sex and I wasn't going to rush her. For one, I was a gentleman. For the other... I would have waited an eternity to sleep with her. The gift of Callie at that time in my life was not her beauty or her body, but her soul.

I wish I had been able to hold onto her.

"Storm's getting worse," she murmurs against my chest.

I follow her gaze to the window. And sure enough, the sky is getting whiter. Soon it will be the only thing we're able to see. I hear the wind whipping outside the window, battering the building, while inside we're as safe as can be, even safer with our arms around each other.

"Oh man…" I mutter, feeling my muscles start to ache.

"Are you okay?" Callie leaps right back into caretaker mode.

I chuckle, trying to readjust. "Just sore."

She retreats from me, sitting up, ready to check every part of my body. "Where are you sore?"

"Callie…" I reach up and touch her cheek. "I'll be fine. Just… relax, would you?"

"But if you're hurt–"

"I'm tired because I just ravished you."

Callie flushes. "*Liam…*"

In this moment, I can see the old Callie. Freshly eighteen, still naïve to how men saw her–demure, lovely with such pure energy. "Didn't I?" I ask with a cocked eyebrow.

Then, she nods firmly. "You did."

"So would you do me a favor and just lie down with me and allow me to bask in this feeling?"

Callie smiles demurely and then tucks herself back into my arm. "How long have you wanted to do that?" she asks.

Ten years. "Since you started being a pain in my ass."

I hear her grin, her lips moving across her teeth. "Since I got here, then."

"To be honest, I never thought we would. I was never going to act on it." I start to trail my hand up and down her arm. "It just…"

"Made sense."

That's not what I was going to say, but it fits. It just made sense to press our bodies together as needily as possible. I'll have to write about an encounter like this in a book. Not exactly this one, but *like* it. I take her wrist and pull her arm into the air. That tattoo. Ever since I saw it, it's haunted me. "Would you tell me about this now?"

Callie tenses her hand into a fist, the veins in her arms bulging out slightly. "Oh. That."

I thread my fingers between hers, relaxing her fist. "You can tell me the truth."

"It's only partly to do with you."

I trace the lines of the tattoo with my other hand.

"Because you gave me daisies before you broke my heart."

Hearing her say it out loud brings a pang to my heart.

"And I wanted some control. Something. Because when you left, I didn't even have a say in the matter."

"I had to go, Callie, I—"

"I know you did," she says, her blue eyes glimmering. She's a woman now. She understands reality. "But still. I didn't have a say. The flowers wouldn't have kept. So, I put them on my arm." Then she adds pointedly, "Not as a reminder of you. But as a reminder of the things I've been through. The things I'll go through again."

I pull her hand to my mouth and kiss it.

"I don't know, it's kind of silly saying it out loud to you."

"It's not silly. It's beautiful."

She smiles gratefully.

I roll onto my side so I can face her. "Can I tell you something?"

She rolls to mirror me. "Okay."

I'm trying not to get distracted by the way her breasts are *right* fucking there and how full they are pressed against the inside of her arm. It's been years since I've been able to go two rounds, but here with Callie, I think I have it in me. "I had to leave."

"Liam, you don't have to go through this again. Okay? I'm over it."

"No, listen to me," I say, pulling her body close to mine. "I had to do it. I had to end things."

Callie's brows knit together. She doesn't want to talk about it. But I need her to know the truth.

"Nathan found out."

Her eyes widen. "What?"

"Not the whole extent of it. But he found out." I swallow. "Because I told him."

A younger Callie might push me away in frustration. But this Callie, the one I've just made love to in my bed, just wants to understand. "W-why?"

"Because I..." I can't believe I'm telling her this. "Because I wanted to be with you. And I wouldn't have been able to pursue anything with you without Nathan knowing."

She stares at me in disbelief.

"So, I told him that we'd both talked about a mutual attraction. Nothing more. And he knew we'd been spending time together. And the moment I asked, it just pissed him off. You know how hard it is to get your brother mad."

Callie nods. "It's like getting Winne the Pooh mad."

"Exactly. Doesn't happen often but when it does, you don't want to be there."

Callie laughs lightly and then touches my cheek. "You seriously told him?"

"I did. I'm sorry."

"No, that's..." She gives me a small smile. "That's nice to know, Liam. I felt crazy when you walked away. So it's nice to know that you gave a shit."

I nudge my nose against Callie's cheek. "Of course, I gave a shit."

If things weren't complicated *once again*, I'd happily ask her if she wanted to try for real this time. But we're bogged down by a contract. Not to mention her brother is still her brother. And even though it's been ten years, I can't imagine his ire would be any less.

"Nate never said anything to me," Callie says.

"Of course, he didn't. You're his precious little sister." I kiss her softly. "As it should be." *As you'll always be.*

While Nate and I might be in a perpetual game of phone tag, he's the best friend I have. I can't lose him. As much as I want Callie in every way, shape, and form,

I've got to make sacrifices here and there. Besides, I won't be able to find a nurse I like nearly as much.

"Would you want to do that again some time?" Callie asks with a suggestive lilt, tapping her fingers against my chest.

"You mean..." I push my hips up against her.

She laughs. "Yes. I do mean that." She tucks some of my hair behind my ear and touches my chin. "You know, just that. No strings. No obligations. Just... sex."

"What happened to sweet innocent Callie, huh?" I tease.

"Oh, Liam, she grew up. She grew *way*, way up," Callie replies with a haggard sigh. Only twenty-eight and life has already done a number on her.

I get it. That's the way it goes. "Friends with benefits, hm?"

She shrugs, eyes rolling upward with mischief. "We could call it that."

I start to trail kisses from her shoulder up to her neck. "And no one... ever... has to... know."

A giggle peels out from between her lips. Her body jerks in my arms, reminding my length how hard it can get if she rubs me just the right way. "Exactly. Our little secret."

"Okay. Our little secret." A big fucking secret, if you ask me. I would love to shout to the world I'm fucking Callie Emerson, but I can't. Because it's our little secret.

Callie kisses me softly on the lips. "I'm going to use the bathroom."

"And then?"

She rolls away from me and sits at the edge of the bed. "And then I'll come back."

"And then?"

She glances over her shoulder at me like a coy femme fatale. "You tell me."

I wrap my arms around her waist and pull her back into my arms. "Well, if I had my way..." I press my lips to hers.

"Yes...?"

"I'd do that all again," I growl. "And it'd feel even better the second time."

Callie practically purrs. God, this woman is a marvel. "You promise?"

"Promise, baby."

"Then the sooner you let me go, the sooner you can make good on that."

Reluctantly, I release Callie from my arms. I admire all the curves and edges of her naked body as she crosses to the bathroom. She glances back at me. "Like what you see?"

Love. Too big a word for a moment like this. For a relationship like this. "Hurry back so I can fuck you, baby."

Callie giggles gleefully and then disappears into the bathroom.

I roll onto my back, sighing heavily. I can't wait to make good on my promise. She doesn't know the animal that she's unleashed.

But deep down, I know I want to give her more than just my body. I want to give her my soul, too.

Maybe in another life, another world.

In this one, though, we're each other's biggest secret.

And I can live with that. For now.

Chapter 12

Callie

A week of Liam. Not just living with him but *having* him.

I walk around with only one brain cell working and that one brain cell is horny beyond belief. I never tire of our antics. Despite us having sex several times a day, sneaking around behind Wade and Emma's backs, I always want more.

And for not being in tip top form, Liam is as virile as a man could be. I may be a woman of medicine, but I do think that the sex has been good for his morale. Every day that passes, he uses the chair less and less. I've ordered a cane for him, which I know he won't be happy about, but he'll need it for a bit while he continues to build up his strength.

Truth is, he won't need me sooner than later. And despite the few times he's hinted at maybe retaining my services longer, it wouldn't make sense given his condition. He'll be thriving without me in no time.

I need to take advantage of the time that I *do* have.

"What kind of meds is he getting, Cal?" Emma asks me while I help her fold some laundry.

"Ibuprofen. Sometimes Percocet," I say with a shrug. "Although to be honest, he doesn't like taking the prescribed meds."

"Huh."

"Why?"

Emma glances down the hallway toward the library where Liam is taking a phone call. "He just seems... I don't know how to describe it."

I do.

"Happier?"

"You think?" I ask, trying to sound as innocent as possible.

"Oh, come on, he doesn't complain nearly as much about doing his exercises, does he?" Emma says, nudging me with her elbow. "I thought you'd be the first to notice."

I have been, but not for the reasons she thinks. "Well, he's getting better. Maybe he can see the work in action and knows it's going to have an impact on him for the better."

"Callie, you're so sweet. But Mr. Sterling is as stubborn as a mule. There's no way he'd ever admit someone else might be right."

I giggle. "Then maybe I've just done a good job of making him feel like doing his exercises and maintaining a regimen is *his* idea."

Emma snickers. "Can you teach me how to do that with my dad? Because if Mr. Sterling is as stubborn as a mule, my papi is–"

Wade pops his head into the hallway. "Callie? Frederick's calling. Says there's something for you downstairs."

I frown. "Huh?"

"Yeah. Flowers or something."

"Oooh! Callie! Do you have a Valentine?"

Shit. It's Valentine's Day. I'd done such a good job of pushing it out of my head I'd forgotten about it. Or nearly forgotten about it.

"I don't know who it would be from," I say carefully as I walk down the hall. "But alright."

As I ride the elevator down, my mind runs through all the possibilities. There is of course, the obvious. Liam. I had set my expectations low. After all, Liam and I are just having fun. That doesn't merit any sort of Valentine's Day celebration.

It's also possible that it's something from my mom. She's always keen on celebrating holidays. Or maybe Nate? But I've been careful not to give him this address. I opened a P.O. box for this exact reason.

When I arrive in the lobby, Frederick is waiting for me, holding a bundle of the reddest roses I've ever seen. "Oh, my goodness!" I exclaim as he shoves them into my arms as if it's a newborn. It certainly weighs the same as a newborn.

"Just delivered for you, Ms. Emerson. Clearly, you have an admirer."

There's a card situated amidst the buds. I practically snatch it out in excitement and open it.

xxx, Kaminsky

I smile to myself. "I guess so. Thank you."

I hurry back upstairs, my mind rushing with thoughts. That sneak. Ordering me flowers when I haven't got anything for him. Not to mention the three x's; a double entendre if I know Liam at all. Both kisses and something more lascivious.

I tuck the card into the pocket of my scrubs and head back inside.

"Red roses?! From who?!" Emma immediately shrieks upon seeing me.

"I don't know, there wasn't a card," I say, carrying them into the kitchen where Wade is working on lunch.

"So, you have no idea who would have sent you flowers? None at all?" Emma asks incredulously.

I shake my head.

"You haven't been on a Tinder date recently?"

I laugh. "Who has the time when keeping up with Liam Sterling?"

Wade points to me with his knife. "Good point."

"Give these to me. I'm going to figure it out." Emma snatches the flowers out of my hand and brings them over to the sink. "Wade, I need your knife for the thorns."

Wade sighs. "Coming..."

Wade and Emma begin pouring over the flowers with everything in them, taking each stem out and depositing them into a vase. They're busy. I have other things on my mind.

Like thanking the man who got me flowers when he wasn't supposed to and now could be attracting suspicion.

I creep down the hallway to the library. The door is closed, but Liam's given me permission to barge in at any point. In the name of medicine and/or lust. I can hear he's already started his phone call. But I can't help it. I need to get what's mine. I pop open the door. Liam is sitting in his leather easy chair, legs extended outward.

"Yeah, I'll need about six weeks there, I think," Liam says, eyeing me curiously.

I close the door behind me and smile.

"No, no. No guide. I don't want a guide. The character wouldn't have a guide."

I cross to where he's sitting and stand over him, tucking my hands behind my back.

A cocked smile appears on his lips. "Security, of course," he says into the phone. "But no guides. It's inauthentic that way."

I lean my hands onto his knees, drawing closer to him.

"Yeah, listen, Ron, I think I'm–" I interrupt him with a soft kiss to his lips. "I think I'm going to have to call you back, I'm..." I kiss him again, pulling myself onto the chair to straddle him. Liam holds back a moan in his throat. "Yes, something's just, ehem, popped up and–"

I hold back a laugh as I trail a line of kisses down from his mouth to his jaw, to his neck to his shoulder. That thing that's just popped up is getting hard between my legs.

"I'll call you right back. Okay... okay, Ron. Buh-bye. Yeah, bye." Liam hangs up the phone and grabs the sides of my face, kissing me deeply on the mouth. "What the hell was that about?" he asks breathlessly as he draws away.

I giggle. "I'm just thanking you. For the flowers."

"In the middle of my phone call?" he asks.

"Couldn't wait." I kiss him softly again. "You know I'm a very impatient girl."

Liam hums with pleasure. "They're not daisies, but..."

"No, they're perfect. They're perfect..." I murmur, sliding my hands down his chest to the waistband of his sweats.

His head dips back. "Oh, shit."

"I haven't even done anything yet."

"But I know what you're about to do, Callie, and that's..." He growls to himself. "That's enough to get me..."

I interrupt him with a kiss. "Seriously, Liam. Thank you."

He smiles. "You like them?"

"Love them. Wade and Emma love them too. They're trying to figure out who sent them to me right now."

"Oh?"

"Yes, but I..." I pull the note out of my pocket. "I have the evidence." I bring my other hand lower. "X...x...x..."

Liam chuckles. "I thought you'd like that."

I start to wrap my hand around his length, but he grabs my wrist.

"Before you do that, I want to ask you something."

"*Then* can I have it?"

"That and more Callie." He pauses, locking eyes with me. "My next book. I need to travel to do some research."

My insides seize. "When?"

"Month or so."

I shake my head. "Liam, that's too soon."

"I want you to come with me."

Talk about whiplash. I've just been ready to rip him a new one and now he's asking me to come with him on a trip to– where is he going anyway?

"Then you can keep an eye on me. Take care of me."

"Where are you going?"

"Egypt."

"Oh my God, Liam," I sigh. "That's a lot."

His hands travel up my back and I have to resist the urge to swoon. I ignore my instincts. "I know it's a lot. But it's my job, Callie."

"You're not ready."

"I am! I'm practically walking already."

I scoff. "That's not good enough." It's his life, his body. I'm just his nurse. But I have to admit I'm definitely acting out of fear. I don't want him to get hurt again, and I don't want him to leave me so soon.

"Callie, would you trust me?" he asks, cradling my cheeks in his hands. "I know my body."

I glance down into the v of his t-shirt and chew on my lower lip. I'm starting to know his body, too.

"Come with me."

I shake my head. "I have to think about it."

Liam is silent for a moment. He clearly expected me to say yes. But I've worked hard for this career. Liam just happened to be a speedbump along the way. I can't just throw it all away and leave New York to be his personal nurse or... something else. Maybe something more?

Don't go there Callie. Friends with benefits. Nothing more.

"Are you upset with me?" he asks.

I inhale sharply and force a smile. "No." I kiss him harshly and grind my hips against him. I want to put the idea of Egypt far from my mind. "Right now, I need you."

Liam laughs against my lips. "You've got me."

Chapter 13

Liam

I'm starting to worry. Callie left over an hour ago to grab some painkillers from Duane Reed. Somehow, I've run low on ibuprofen and now I have a migraine. It shouldn't have taken her more than half an hour. And it's getting later by the minute, already closing in on half past ten. Wade and Emma are already long gone for the day.

Of course, she's a free woman. She can do as she pleases.

But she can't worry me. I can't stand to be worried.

I look down at my phone at the unanswered text I sent her. On the seldom occasion Callie leaves the house, whether it be for a quick errand or a visit with a friend, she's usually quite responsive. Especially since we've started our affair.

The past few weeks, my attraction to her has grown in every direction. It started off as a desperation for her body and her touch. Now, I have the aching need to take care of her, just as she has done for me.

I know our agreement. Just sex. But we should have known that'd be impossible given that we practically live together. I spend almost all of my waking moments with her. And when I'm away from her, I long for her.

Every bit of her.

It's getting bad.

I call down to the front desk. It wouldn't surprise me if Frederick was holding her hostage in a friendly conversation. Wouldn't be the first time.

"Mr. Sterling, how can I help you?" Frederick's cheerful voice comes through the phone.

"Has Callie been by?"

"Oh, no, Mr. Sterling." His tone is immediately grave. "Is everything alright?"

I sigh. "I hope so. I just was expecting her back sooner than later."

"Well, I'll keep an eye out for her sir." He pauses. "I'm sure she's fine."

I bite my lower lip. I'm not convinced, but I'm going to try and remain optimistic. She'll be back. I know she will be. "Thanks, Frederick."

"Any time, sir."

I hang up the phone look out the tall window of my library. I've been sitting in my easy chair reading a book, biding my time until Callie returns. The darkness of New York City is never truly dark, even on the top floor. There are always lights somewhere in the sky, masquerading as stars, obscuring nature's celestial bodies.

I can't wait to get to Egypt and get out of the penthouse. I just hope Callie will come with me. I know she's worried about my walking which is even more reason she should come. If Nate catches wind that she's my nurse... It's work. Nothing's happening.

Although, in my heart, I wish something more would happen.

I can only daydream about adventures on the Nile with Callie for so long before I remember the time. I check my phone again. Each second that passes feels like a second closer to losing her, another reason that something might be wrong.

I have to do something.

I push myself up from the chair and hobble to the front of the apartment, wielding my cane. When Callie showed it to me, I'd outright refused to use it. But it was that or the chair. And I have to admit, I don't get as tired when I use it.

From the hall closet, I rip my coat off a hanger and slide it on, already one foot out the door.

The ride down in the elevator is painfully slow. I tap my cane on the ground. "Come on, come *on*."

The doors finally open and I stride out into the elevator as best I can. Frederick's eyes shoot to me, to my cane. I haven't been seen outside the apartment with it and I'm suddenly very embarrassed.

"Mr. Sterling! It's so wonderful to see you on your feet!" he announces with a grin.

I'd like nothing more than to melt into the earth of embarrassment. However, there's no time for that. "I'm going out to find Callie. If I'm not back in—"

As if I have spoken her into existence, the doors out to the street fly open and Callie appears. From just one glance, I know something's wrong. Her coat has been torn asunder and it looks like down is poking out of her side. Her blonde hair has tumbled out of the claw clip at the back of her head. And her eyes... God, there's terror in those eyes.

Without hesitation, I rush to her as fast as I can. "Callie, what's wrong?"

"Liam..." she says, voice tiny and full of relief.

I grab her by the arms and pull her further into the lobby. "What's wrong? Oh my God, you're shaking."

"I was... my purse," Callie says through tight breaths. "Some man attacked me and he got my purse." Her hands tighten around my jacket. "He had as knife."

I touch the side of her jacket where the down is spilling out her coat. No blood. It was just a threat. Thank God. "Frederick, call the police."

"Already on it, sir," Frederick says from behind the desk, phone already against his ear.

"Are you hurt?" I ask her. I touch the side of her head. "Did he hurt you?"

She shakes her head. "I don't think so."

"Good," I reply and pull her into my chest tightly. "Good."

I've thrown all caution to the wind. I don't care who sees me holding her. I can't help but feel responsible. She went out there for me. Something could have happened to her. She could have been hurt. She could have been killed.

"I should have known better than to let you go out there," I whisper, lowering my lips to the crown of her head.

Callie doesn't reply. Her whole body has been taken over by shock.

"Come here, sit down," I say and lead her over to the sitting area of the lobby. As soon as I have her seated, I grab her a cup of water from a dispenser near the elevator. There are various fruits mingling in the water; their party seems inappropriate for the moment but it's the best I can do. I return to Callie and hand her the cup. "Here, drink this."

Callie accepts it gratefully and sips the icy water bit by bit. I sit across from her on an ottoman, observing every part of her.

Back in the day, on the rig, injuries were common. A few deaths, too. Heavy machinery was an accepted hazard of the job. But while injuries were dealt with immediately by medical personnel, there were always the brushes with danger. Those were sometimes even scarier and could make a guy dissociate for an entire week, eyes glazed over, playing out just how one minute of difference could have cost him his life.

I see that in Callie now, her eyes so wide it's like she's trying to see into the past and remember every detail.

"It's okay," I whisper to her, touching her knees tenderly. Her body flinches at my touch, but then settles when she remembers it's me. "You're safe."

Callie swallows and nods.

"Police are on their way, Mr. Sterling," Frederick calls out from across the lobby.

"Thank you, Frederick," I say. Though my heart is still pounding, I'm trying to remain strong for Callie. I'll keep a stiff upper lip, tense jaw. I'll be her rock. I'll be anything for her.

Callie reaches out and touches the zipper of my coat. "You were leaving."

"I was coming to find you," I say.

A subtle smile appears on her lips as she notices the cane I've leaned against the ottoman beside me.

"I had texted you, but you weren't responding and–"

She reaches into her pocket and produces her phone. "It's dead. I tried to call for help, but it was–"

"It's okay. I knew something was wrong," I murmur and touch her cheek softly.

Callie's eyes flutter shut. A glass tear slides down her cheek.

"I'm so sorry, Callie."

"It's not your fault," she says in a choked voice.

"It is. I shouldn't have asked you to go out there."

"You needed something for your head."

In my worry, I've totally forgotten about my headache. I've been so focused on Callie that I've forgotten about my own pain. "It wasn't worth this. I would have managed."

She sighs and falls into my chest. I wrap her up in my arms. I need her to know that I'm here to protect her. I'll never let anyone hurt her. Never again.

Because she's...

She's my whole world. That's become more and more clear every day.

"I don't know what I would have done if I'd lost you," I say softly. Forget the rules. Forget the agreement. I need her to know.

Callie grips my jacket as if to bury herself in my chest.

"Mr. Sterling."

I look up to Frederick. He gestures toward the door. Red and blue lights are bouncing through the windows from the street. "The police are here."

"Thank God," I breathe a sigh of relief.

I start to get up, but Callie holds tightly to me. "Don't go."

"I won't, I won't."

Her blue eyes are glassy as they look up into mine. "Don't leave me. I can't be alone."

All I was going to do was meet the police at the door. But it's clear that Callie needs me in every way she can possibly have me. "I'm right here," I whisper. "I won't leave your side."

And I don't. The police come and question Callie, ask for her statements and what was missing. The entire time I sit at her side, holding her hand, encouraging her as the words come out stifled and strange.

There's a part of me that wants to go out there and find the piece of shit myself. I don't care if I don't have the strength to run or that my dominant hand is still a little weak and tingly.

No one will ever hurt Callie Emerson.

Not on my watch.

Chapter 14

Callie

It feels like a bad dream, but when I wake up in Liam's arms, it all comes flooding back to me.

It was terrifying and so fast I didn't even have time to breathe. I was walking out of Duane Reed with the migraine medication in my pocket, hunkered down like a turtle in my coat. The only other person around was walking down the street approaching me faster and faster until suddenly they were upon me, struggling with me for my purse, knife against the outer shell of my jacket.

I let him have it and ran as fast as my legs would carry me back home, back to Liam.

And he was so...

He was so good to me. Didn't even flinch for a second while my body succumbed to a terror I had never known.

I don't remember much of what happened after I got home. But I do remember Liam at my side every step of the way.

"Callie," Liam whispers in a groggy voice, waking.

"Hm?"

"You're awake."

I nestle myself back into him, his whole body spooning me from behind. We don't sleep together every night. In fact, we resist it. After all, that's a step past just sex, isn't it? That's intimate. That's closeness.

And God, how I want to be close to him.

I plant a kiss to his forearm.

"How are you feeling?"

If I'm honest, I never want to leave the house ever again. I know that feeling will fade with time, but for now, the only place I can imagine feeling safe is right here in Liam's arms. "I'm okay."

Liam nuzzles his nose into my hair and kisses the back of my head. "Good." His arms tighten around me.

I slide my hand into his weak one. It's getting stronger by the day. I can feel it just in the way our fingers interlock. "Thank you."

"Mm. For what?"

A thousand things come to mind. For protecting me. For holding me. For trying to keep me safe. For giving me something that feels like love. Instead I answer, "Just for being there."

Callie, no. You know better than this. This isn't how this ends.

Each day I spend with Liam has just been another steppingstone toward loving him. Despite his original edgy demeanor, he's worked himself back into my heart, just as he was ten years ago.

And ten years ago, I loved him. I just never said it out loud.

I'm feeling all of that again, though. I'm gripped by the terrifying feeling of my whole heart expanding to let another person in.

You can't do this, Callie. You know how it ended the first time.

But what if this is my second chance?

"Did you sleep alright?" Liam asks, leaning himself up on his elbow.

I look up into his warm brown eyes and smile. "Better than expected." I run my hand over his stubbled cheek. "Better with you next to me."

Liam cracks a smile, flushing slightly. "Callie..."

I know where he's going. "Don't."

"I'm sorry."

"Liam, please."

"I can't help it, what if something –"

"Nothing did."

"But–"

I look him hard in the eye. "Nothing happened, Liam."

He furrows his brow, examining my face closely. "What would I have told your brother?"

"Don't bring my brother into the bed," I say with a half-hearted laugh.

His arms tighten around me, hands grabbing at the soft parts of me. Not because he needs my body. But because he needs me close. As close as possible. "What would I have done? What would I have told him about us?"

About us? "You wouldn't have had to tell him about us."

"Callie..." Liam begins carefully. "What if I wanted to tell him about us?"

I stare at him. Is this a confession? "Do you want to tell him about us?"

He swallows. I watch his Adam's apple bob. "I don't know."

There's no world where Nate would understand. Where he wouldn't feel so deeply hurt and betrayed. There's no reason my brother should know.

Unless... we were something more than what we'd agreed upon.

"I just know that I want you," Liam murmurs, his eyes falling to my mouth.

Want is a big word. I know he wants my body. Maybe more.

I want the same.

I close the space between us, kissing him hard. A long, winding kiss that seems to last infinitely. Liam pulls my body as close to him as possible. If I was any closer, I'd be a part of him.

"Do you want me, Callie?" Liam whispers against my mouth.

"Yes."

"Yeah?"

"Yes. All of you." And I mean it. From the tips of his toes to the top of his head, from his deepest thoughts to his most tremulous feelings, I want all of Liam... for a long fucking time.

I slide my arms around him, now face to face on the bed, and throw my leg over his hips. I can feel him already edging into hardness between my legs.

"First," Liam says breathlessly, "I want you in my mouth."

I moan.

"Can I have you in my mouth Callie?"

I only manage to nod. The thought of his tongue ensnaring my clitoris has made me exponentially wetter.

Liam slides down the bed, pressing kisses against the front of my body: my clavicle, my breasts, my belly, and then the crest of my pubic bone. "I can smell you," he growls. Liam hooks his arms under my thighs. All of his movements are gentle. "I want to take care of you, Callie." He licks my labia, teasing the hidden sensitive parts underneath. My hips jolt. "I want to please you."

"You please me..." I say with a tender smile.

Liam looks me in the eye as he works his tongue between my lower lips and then ensnares my clit in his mouth. I buck unintentionally and swear under my breath.

He works my pussy as if he's kissing me. Hums against it as if it's the most delicious thing he's ever tasted. His hands splay out across my pelvis. From time to time, he glances up at me to make sure I'm enjoying myself and, dear Lord, am I enjoying myself.

With each flick of his tongue, I feel a warm zap to my trembling center. My nerves are starting to catch fire. I grip the pillow behind my head and begin to thrust my hips against him, fucking his face like he's inside me.

Liam groans against me, his limp hand struggling to hold onto my thigh. But he's enjoying every second of it.

I don't know what's coming over me, but I feel like I might burst into tears. It's not just pleasure. There's something else happening inside me.

"Stop, stop," I exclaim suddenly.

He listens without question, raising his head and widening his eyes. "What's wrong, are you alright?"

"I don't..." I try to catch my breath. "I don't want to come yet."

Liam frowns.

"I need you inside me Liam," I say, almost on the edge of tears. "I need you... inside. *Now.*"

With concern in his eyes, Liam lifts himself up from my legs. My essence glistens across his chin and cheeks.

"Please," I add, almost pathetically.

Liam's eyes are locked with mine as he crawls back up the length of my body. He glances down at my bare breasts and aching pussy, before his eyes land on mine again.

I wrap my hand around the base of his neck. "Look me in the eyes as you go inside me."

His eyebrows jump, but he follows my request, pushing his cock into my soft wet center, eyes never leaving mine.

"Oh my God," I gasp as I watch his pupils dilate.

"Damn, you feel so good," Liam says, trying with everything in him not to look away. "You feel so..."

We remain there, just our parts locked together, relishing in the closeness. I cup his chin in my hand. "Liam, I..."

Don't say it. Your hormones are raging. You don't actually feel anything. You don't love this man.

"I want to be on top of you."

He half-laughs and nods. "I'd like nothing better."

With aching slowness, we roll together so I'm straddling Liam's hips. I lower myself further onto him, listening to his strained whimper. I start to rock back and forth on top of him.

His hands slide up my thighs to my lower back. "Do what you gotta do, Callie."

And while I can feel compounding pleasure in my belly, my emotions feel even bigger. My eyes are starting to prick with tears and the sounds coming from my mouth sound more like whimpers than moans.

I fall forward and grip the sheets on either side of his head for more leverage, thrusting faster. "Feels... so... good." I shut my eyes, feel tears start to spill down my cheeks.

"Oh, God yes, Callie." Liam claps his hands against my ass cheeks and squeezes. "You're so fucking good."

I drop my head and move as fast as I can while taking Liam as deep as he'll go. Our breath comes in hiccupping spurts.

"Shit, you're gonna make me –"

"*Look at me.*" I grip Liam's head and force his eyes into mine. I don't care that I'm crying, that my eyes are red and my face is slick. "See what you do to me? Do you fucking see?"

His brow folds as he attempts to discern my expression.

"You make me feel *so good*," I sob.

"This is because you feel good, Callie?" he asks, softly touching the tracks of my tears.

"*Yes.*" I blink, several tears falling onto the plane of his chest.

Liam pushes some of my hair behind my ear and then pulls me into him. "Come here. Stop working so hard and lay here with me."

With his cock still buried hard inside me, I fall into Liam's chest and weep. He rubs my back gently and coos to me, "It's alright, it's alright. I've got you."

How I wish I could tell him everything running through my mind. How my whole life is on fire for him.

Then, he pushes his lips against my ear, "You make me feel so good too."

And whether he means it or not, I feel like he's saying what I'm thinking. There is something more here. More than just secret rendezvous and sex.

"You make me feel..." Liam starts to move his hips into me, soft and slow. "Like no woman has ever made me feel."

"Oh, Liam," I whisper. Even these subtle movements are making my g-spot throb.

"And I want to make you feel like no man has ever made you feel," he continues, his pace quickening.

I push my face into his neck and hook my arms under him, grabbing his shoulders. I'm so close.

"Like no man... will ever make you feel... again..." Grunts interrupt his words, clenched teeth attempting to hold back a torrent of expletives and moans.

He pounds up into me fast and strong until both of us are barely holding on by a thread. The room goes silent for a split second before fire whips through my body and I cry out into his hair with pleasure.

I feel him explode inside me. He grabs me hard, fingers making indents in my skin like they're tattoos.

Liam lets out a long growl as my pussy milks him, clenching around him, drawing out every last bit of his euphoria.

I hold onto him as tight as I can.

I never want another man ever again.

The only man I want is Liam.

But before either of us can say anything or even begin to come down from our high, his bedside phone rings.

"The phone–"

"Leave it," he spits. He embraces me tight and breathes in the scent of my neck. "Leave it…"

The ring is painful, each one growing in urgency. Finally, the voicemail picks up.

"Mr. Sterling, it's Frederick. There's a guest down here to see you. Says he's an old friend of yours. Nate Emerson. I've sent him up."

My heart sinks.

Chapter 15

Liam

Nate Emerson is downstairs. And I'm quite literally inside his sister.

Callie's eyes shoot into mine. "What the hell."

"I had no idea he–"

"*What the hell, Liam.*" Callie pushes herself up, leaving me and my body behind. "Why didn't you tell me?"

My body feels freezing cold without her close. "*Me???* I didn't know he was coming!"

"Well, I didn't either! He doesn't even know I'm here!"

"Right, exactly. How could either of us have known then?"

"Why did Frederick just send him up?? What if–"

I sigh. "Your last name. He probably just assumed or... God I hope he didn't say anything that would –"

Callie pushes her hands over her face. "Oh my god..."

Silence falls over the room. Just beyond these walls, I know the elevator is already creeping up, higher and higher, coming with our doom. "Okay. You need to go."

Her eyes flick to mine, trembling.

I push myself up from the bed, grabbing my cane and robe. "Go to your room and get changed. Grab some of your things. You're going to need to find somewhere to go until we can figure this out." I'd like nothing more than to say screw it and just have Nate find out the truth about Callie and me. But we haven't even discussed it. Sure, it seemed clear in our bodies. That was the best sex of my life, and I can only hope hers too.

You don't have sex like that with someone you're *just* fucking.

It's deeper than that.

"We need to make sure there's no sign of you in the apartment," I say, rushing to grab her coat and shoes from the front hall.

Callie follows suit, making a sweep of the main room.

"What are you going to say?" Callie calls out.

"I'm just going to play it cool, now you go and–"

A knock at the door. *Shit*. "Liam *Sterling*!" Nate's voice playfully resonates through the door. "It's moi! Your old pal!"

Callie and I lock eyes. I hate to cast her out like this. But we have no choice. "*Go*," I say in a tight whisper.

"How am I going to get out if–"

"We'll figure it out," I say.

Callie sighs. I want nothing more than for her to reach out and kiss me. Let me know that casting her out like this hasn't changed anything between us.

Fear, however, is more potent at this moment. As quick as a flash, she runs down the hall to her room. As soon as I hear her door snap shut, I know it's time.

I limp over to the door, holding my head high.

Calm down, Liam. It's just Nate. He has no idea Callie is here and has no reason to be suspicious.

I grip the door handle.

"Yoo-hoo! Liaaaaam!" his voice comes through the door again.

Now or never, buddy. And it has to be now.

I open the door, letting it swing all the way open. Nothing to hide in here.

Nate Emerson. In the flesh. Same blonde hair and blue eyes as Callie. If the guilt hadn't set in already, now it's consuming me. "Shit, you've got a cane and everything," he remarks with a lopsided grin.

The thing about Nate is he never fails to make me smile. That's what drew me to him on the rig. I was hardened and tired of working my ass off for two weeks at a time in the middle of the ocean. And he came in with his grin and the gap between his two top teeth, always ready with a joke and a smile. Not sure why he gravitated toward me and my grumpiness, but I have always been grateful for it.

I could probably stand to act like I'm more grateful for it once and awhile. And that would probably start with *not* sleeping with his sister.

"I'm sorry, I'm looking for Liam Sterling? You look like him, but much more *rugged*," he says, gesturing to my face and hair.

"Oh, it's me. Just..." I say. I clock a small rolling suitcase at his side. "This is a surprise."

"Why are you acting like you've seen a ghost? Come here, man."

Nate wraps me into a big hug. Though he's a bit shorter than me, he's always been stronger. Denser muscular build. And I have to say, it's nice to give my old buddy a hug. "How long's it been? Years?" Nate asks, clapping his hand on my back. Then, he draws away, hands on my shoulders. "You know, I was expecting you to look a lot worse than this."

"Gee, thanks."

"You know what I mean."

"What are you doing here, Nate?"

Nate laughs almost incredulously. "I'm here to surprise you buddy. I know you've been cooped up; thought you might need a little company."

Classic Nate, so sweet and giving. Not realizing what everyone else is doing behind his back.

He nervously glances at the suitcase. "Don't worry, I've got my own hotel room, you don't have to put me up, I just –"

"No, that's ridiculous." Not only is Nate visiting but he's going to be my houseguest. *Great.* "There's no reason for you to stay anywhere but here."

He smiles gratefully. "Awesome."

I don't know what more to say. The longer I stand in the doorway, the more time I'm buying Callie. But I've run out of ways to distract at this moment in time because my mind keeps traveling to my dick that's still covered in her.

"Can I come in?"

You can't think about fucking Callie while you're staring right at Nate, jackass. "Of course," I say, stepping aside.

As soon as Nate walks in, his suitcase rolling behind him, I feel like I've invited him into a minefield. At any moment he could tread upon a mine that would make the whole room explode. I have to be careful.

"Let me get you a drink, huh?" I say, shepherding him directly into the kitchen.

"Oh, just water is good for me. Just got off a plane, you know how dehydrating those things can be."

"Do I ever." I grab him a glass and go to the fridge to pour him a cup of water. Immediately, I am face to face with the list of medications and rules in Callie's handwriting. I rip it down covertly as I can and crumple them into my pocket.

"I have to say, I couldn't believe your doorman let me up without even letting you know. You know, this was supposed to be a *surprise*." Nate leans against the counter. "Unless you're psychic and I never knew it."

I force a chuckle and hand Nate a glass of water. "No, I have a shortlist of people who are welcome anytime." It's a lie, but not a bad idea.

Nate grins brightly. "I made the shortlist? Little ole' me?"

"You're one of my best friends, Nate." *Even if I don't act like it most of the time.* "Of course, you're welcome any time."

"Well, then maybe you can host me and the girls for summer vacation. I've always wanted to bring them to New York."

"Of course."

Nate rolls his eyes. "Kidding buddy. I'm kidding."

I stare at him, unable to figure out what to say next.

"Gimme a tour, huh?" Nate turns, abandoning his suitcase, and saunters out into the living room.

I rush after him, not paying any mind to the tension throbbing in my legs. "If I had known you were coming, I would have cleaned up but –"

"You're not going to make excuses for your New York penthouse, man," Nate says with a laugh. "You don't even want to see my house. Everywhere you turn, you're liable to step on a Lego."

"Right, well." I follow him into the living room. "This is the living area."

"Damn, look at that view." Nate strides directly over to the windows and looks out at the view, crossing his arms. "No wonder you write so many books every year. This view must be inspiring."

I chuckle. "You're right about that."

Nate turns on his heels suddenly. "Ooh, what's back here?"

He walks toward the hallway and my heart starts to race. "Wait, wait. If I had known you were coming, I could have had a room made up for you, but–"

"Relax man. I'm just curious about your digs." He opens the door to the library without even blinking. This guy really sometimes lacks a sense of decorum. I thank God it wasn't Callie's room. "Shit, look at all these books!"

I follow him to the doorway, making sure the stand in his way in case he wants to dart out and go open other doors without knocking. "It's nice, isn't it?"

Nate wanders around the library, lots of questions on his lips. I do my best to answer them, but my ear is turned toward the room just down the hall where I can imagine Callie is all packed and ready to go, cowering near the door, waiting for her opportunity.

Out of the corner of my eye, I see a crack in her door. She peeks out, only one of her blue eyes visible.

I shake my head minutely and hold my finger up. *Nearly there, Callie.*

She nods and pulls the door closed again.

"Hey, let me show you to your room, huh?" I announce loudly.

Nate looks away from a shelf full of antique copies of Dickens. "Only if there are mints on my pillow."

"I can arrange that with my housekeeper." I step aside. "Follow me."

I walk down the hall carefully. "So, I've got a few extra rooms. There's also a media room which I mostly use for research or screening adaptations of my books, which are usually cringe inducing at best, but –"

"And this is?"

I flip around and see his hand on the door to Callie's room. "Don't!"

Nate retracts his hand as if he's been burnt by the metal.

"My nurse. That's her room."

"A nurse... I didn't know you had a nurse."

I swallow. "Yes, well, rehab on my legs and hand. She has the week off, though. So. She's out of town."

Nate nods. "Ah..."

"Here, you go ahead, right around the corner is your room. En suite bathroom and everything," I say pointing past the laundry room to the bend in the hallway.

Nate excitedly walks past and once he's out of sight, I turn the knob of Callie's door and open it the slightest bit to let her know the coast is clear. Without looking back, I hurry down the hallway to meet him. Though I know she's being as quiet as a mouse, I can hear her moving down the hall, my senses heightened from fear.

"You want me to do this laundry while I'm here?" Nate asks with a grin, pointing to a basket of laundry on the bed.

"Shit, sorry, man, sometimes my housekeeper uses this room to –"

"I'm just yanking your chain man," Nate laughs. "We have a ping pong table in the basement that my wife has commandeered as the laundry table. I get it."

I smile at the thought of it. Though his life sounds crowded and messy, I like the idea of having a little family that you have to bend your life around. That's what I expected my life to look like at one point.

Now, I'm just alone, nursing wounds from ski accidents on expensive vacations I took with people I don't much care about.

"Well, well, well..." Nate peeks into the basket and pulls out a red thong. I know it to be Callie's. "How old did you say your nurse was?'

"Don't get any ideas."

He laughs, tossing the thong back in the basket. "Me? I'm a married man. I'd never. I mean for you, Liam. She cute?"

"Well, yeah."

"You like her?"

"I do, but–"

"I'm just saying... you never know what could happen," Nate says with a twinkle in his eye.

I try not to grimace outwardly.

No, Nate. You *never know what could happen.*

Chapter 16

Callie

My heart doesn't stop beating until the door closes on the 6 train. I need to get as far from the Upper East Side as possible.

I text Sasha, praying that I get the service I need underground.

Can I crash with you for a couple days?

She responds almost immediately.

Everything okay?

I glance around the subway car. A combination of paranoia and anxiety. First my attack last night and now my brother showing up out of the blue. It's like the universe is trying to shake me awake.

Crazy story. Will tell you when I get to you.

Three dots.

I'll be home. Bring bagels.

I smile to myself and then slip my phone in my bag. Thank God for Apple Pay and virtual MTA passes. I cancelled all my cards last night and have no idea when I'll get any of that back.

The train rocks me calm. I feel like all my nerves have been on high alert since last night. Even while making love with Liam, I was on fire.

I'm terrified of what this means for us. Ten years ago, when faced with this situation, he broke my heart. Now, here's Nate, making us both come face to face with the betrayal. I don't see why he wouldn't do exactly what he did before.

Knowing now also that my brother knew. That Liam *told* him...

God, it would just break Nate's heart.

This situation... it's going to break all our hearts.

I feel my veins pulse in my forearm just thinking about those wild daisies.

The ride on the train back to Brooklyn is the only solace I can find in the consistent rocking and the strange smells, various people piling in, trying to find a seat. From time to time, I find my body stiffening, afraid that someone might come too close, might feel dangerous.

I just need the world to be calm. For just one moment.

Is that too much to ask?

<hr />

"Okay, start again. *What*?"

I chew on my lower lip as I explain to Sasha the situation for the third time over bagels and shmear.

"First of all. Why didn't you tell me your client was Liam *fucking* Kaminsky?" Sasha growls, hands on her hips.

Sasha knows the stories. I've told her all of mine just like she's told me all of hers. She's my closest friend in New York.

But I wanted to keep Liam for me. Plus, if I let the cat out of the bag, who knows how long it would have taken me to spill my guts to Nate? "I just couldn't, Sash."

"I'm your friend!"

"I know, but you would have acted like my friend and either told me to give him a piece of my mind or fuck him and– "

"Would I have been wrong?" Sasha asks indignantly.

I nearly laugh. But this isn't a laughing matter. "No, you wouldn't have been."

"You did both, didn't you?"

"Yes, but–"

She claps her hands. Case closed. "So, you just wanted to be a little bitch then, huh?"

I roll my eyes and collapse into the couch. I can feel the nasty metal bar that pressed into my back for weeks again. This ratty pull-out couch needs to go to the dump. "Sasha, you can't be mad at me right now. I need your help."

Sasha sighs and takes a big bite of her bagel, considering. She swallows. "Fine. I'll reserve my anger. For now."

"Thank you."

"You owe me."

"I know."

She taps her finger against her cheek. "So, Nate's in town."

"Yes."

"And staying with Liam."

"I assume."

"And you've been sleeping with Liam."

"Yes."

"And you've caught feelings for Liam."

I freeze. I haven't said as much to her. But she's my friend. She can see right through me.

She smiles smugly. "Aha..."

"Sash..."

"Oh please, Callie, anyone could have seen that you loved him from a mile away. You've got that tattoo to prove it."

I tense my fist. "The tattoo isn't–"

"Keep telling yourself that, sister." Her warm brown eyes fall onto mine. "We both know the truth."

I feel a knot in my throat. She's right. I know she is. And secretly, the truth has been there all along. I buried it deep in my subconscious and got a tattoo on the inside of my arm thinking that the pain and ink might make my strength permanent.

All it did was confirm one horrible thing.

I love Liam Kaminsky. And I never stopped loving him.

I might have hated him for a time, but that didn't mean my heart didn't still have a place made exactly for him.

"I think you should tell him."

I look to Sasha in alarm. "What?!"

"Your brother. You need to tell him how you feel about Liam."

I look at my bagel. I've barely taken three bites. I'm not even hungry. "*Liam* doesn't even know how I feel about Liam."

"Well, tell him, too. Tell everyone how you feel. Say it out loud right now."

"No."

My friend raises an eyebrow. "Callie…"

"Noooo." I grab a throw pillow and press it to my face. "It's embarrassing."

"Sweetie, love isn't embarrassing."

Oh, but it is. It makes my entire body turn red. How could I have let myself fall to this place. Everyone says love makes you strong, but all it does is make me feel like a pile of jelly on the floor.

"Say, 'I love Li--"

"Fine! Fine." I push the pillow into my lap, gripping it with all my might. "I…" My mouth is dry. "I love…"

"You got it, girl."

"I love L—" My phone starts vibrating loudly on the coffee table. I grab it angrily and look at who's calling. "*Shit.* It's Nate."

Sasha throws up her hands. "These men! Why are they like this?"

I feel the vibrations of the phone pulsing through my hand.

"Just let it ring."

I can't. "I'm not supposed to know he's in town. I always pick up his calls."

Sasha purses her lips and sighs. "Do what you gotta do."

I answer the phone and force a smile on my face. "Natey!"

"Guess what?"

"W-what?"

"I'm in New York!"

I look at Sasha, trying to fake my surprise. "What?! No way!"

"Yeah, I took a few days and thought I'd come visit."

I'm slightly perturbed he's pretending as if he came to see me when in reality his first call was his best friend. "Why didn't you tell me?"

"Well, to be honest, I was coming to visit an old friend who got in an accident recently and he lives..." Nate stops short and then laughs. "You actually know him."

"Oh? I know him?"

Sasha covers her mouth, attempting to stifle a laugh.

"Yeah," Nate says with a sad chuckle. "You remember Liam Kaminsky?"

Hearing him say his name now that I know he knows what was happening ten years ago is the weirdest feeling ever. Now we're all just sweeping things under the rug from each other. "No way! He's in New York!"

"You know the crime author Liam Sterling?"

"*No...*"

"I know! He's made it really big. Penthouse on the Upper East Side and–" I hear a voice cut him off. Liam's voice. Nate laughs at whatever Liam has said and then returns to me, "He's pretending he's modest but when you have this kind of view of Central Park, I think you forgo that privilege."

I try to laugh, but it sounds more like a terrified whimper.

"So listen, I know you're busy with your client– "

Busy is one word for it.

"But I obviously would love to see you and, well, I thought with Liam being in town and you being in town, and *me* now being in town, we should all catch up. Dinner. Old friends, you know?"

My heart sinks. I have no doubt that this entire scheme was Nate's idea. Liam probably fought him tooth and nail. I almost giggle thinking about how that interaction went down.

"Could you make it tonight?"

"Tonight?" I repeat, looking to Sasha for help.

Sasha nods heartily. *Obviously,* she mouths.

"Um, well–"

"Like I said, I know you're busy and I know this is a surprise, but I think it'd be a nice time and–"

"I'll come. What time?"

Sasha flashes me a thumbs up.

"Oh, great! Great. Well, we'll have dinner here. Apparently, Liam has an amazing chef, so–"

God, Wade and Emma. What the hell has Liam told them?

"Let's say about seven? Does that work for you?"

Yeah, what the hell else do I have to do but hang out with my client while pretending he's not my client and also pretending I haven't been sleeping with him? "Sounds perfect. Just send me an address and I'll see you then."

"Oh, great. *Great.*" Nate pulls away from the phone. I hear him say to Liam, "She can make it." And then Liam mutters something in return.

This is all such a crazy mess.

Nate gives me the details. Details I already know about where Liam's apartment is and the name of his doorman and all the other things that are a part of my life that I'm pretending not to know to protect my brother's innocence.

"And Callie?"

"Yeah, Nate?"

"I can't wait to see you."

I feel the love for my brother swell in my chest. I might be pissed he's shown up out of the blue, ruining the heaven Liam and I have been creating, but I have to admit, "I can't wait either."

"Great. Seven. See you then."

Nate hangs up first. I pull the phone from my ear and stare at the screen.

"Jeez, this is a mess," Sasha says, mouthful of bagel.

All I can do is groan and collapse onto the couch.

"You know what we have to do though, right?"

"Hibernate for a thousand years until this all blows over?"

Sasha laughs. "No, silly. We need to get you a kickass, amazing outfit."

I lift my head and eye her.

"After all, even though he *can't* touch you, that doesn't mean he won't *want* to touch you."

She has a point.

"So, bombshell. What do you say?"

A smile creeps across my lips. "I think we're going shopping."

"That's the spirit."

Chapter 17

Liam

"Liam! Callie's here!"

I grab hold of my cane and stare across the living room to the front hallway. This is it. I've been preparing for this all day in my mind.

Look surprised, Liam.

I wrap my hand around the handle of my cane and push myself to standing, grunting to myself. I don't like feeling this old. And without Callie around, I've somehow managed to age ten years in a day. All Nate talks about are his wife and daughters and while I'm happy to hear about it, it just reminds me of my own mortality.

As I limp, slowly and steadily, into the front hall, I hear the reunion. I hear their voices collide and their excited embrace.

Here I come like the big, bad dumbass, ready to interrupt it.

"Let me take your coat," Nate announces.

"Thank you."

I straighten out my button-down. I haven't worn one of these in months. But Nate insisted I dress up. "You haven't seen her in what, ten years?! You need to make a good impression!"

For a split second, it was like he was setting me up on a date. I shook that feeling off quickly.

I know better.

"Liam!"

"I'm coming, I'm..." I step into the front hall and immediately lose my ability to speak.

Callie Emerson is standing in the doorway wearing a green dress that hugs all her curves and shows off the fullness of her breasts perfectly.

Dear god. How does this woman get more beautiful by the day?

She smiles. "Hi, Liam."

I tear my eyes up from her body to her face. She's done her makeup. A full face. I've never seen her in this light. And it's just another beautiful shade of her. With the flicks of liner over her eyes and berry lips, she looks like a very smug cat. She knows what she's doing. She's trying to make this hard for me.

And there's already one part of my body that's hard. So, I guess it's working.

"Callie, it's good to see you." Understatement of the century.

"You too," she says.

Neither of us makes a move to hug for Nate's sake. Even though we don't speak, I can read her body so clearly. This is what happens when you've grown close to someone. Everything about them says something. An unspoken language.

I want to speak her language for the rest of my life.

"Okay, don't be weird, guys," Nate says with a laugh. "Come on, let's go sit."

"Yes, just this way," I say, gesturing into the living room as if she's never been here before.

Callie glances around. She peeks into the kitchen, no doubt searching for Emma and Wade. Little does she know I sent them off an hour ago. Wade's meal for us has been kept warm by a chafing dish in the kitchen.

The three of us are completely alone with nothing but our history to interrupt us.

"You have a beautiful home, Liam," she says with a small smile.

I lean on my cane at the entrance to the living room and nod. "Thank you."

"Liam, tell her about what happened to you. You know, Callie's a nurse. She'd love to hear about all the nitty gritty, I'm sure."

Callie glares at her brother. "*Nate.*"

"Skiing accident," I say with a small smile. I clear my throat. "Perhaps a drink before dinner?"

I pour us all some champagne and, upon handing Callie her glass, I feel her fingers graze mine. Her blue eyes land intensely on mine. "Thank you."

If she only knew how much I wanted to tear her clothes off right then and there... well, I guess we couldn't do anything about it.

But God, how I want her to know.

We all take a seat in the sitting area, me in an armchair and Nate and Callie next to each other on the couch. "So, you're a nurse."

"Yes."

"Where... where do you work?" I ask. I'm a good writer. Not an actor. Hopefully Nate can't see through my act.

"I've actually just transitioned into personal nursing. I'm working with a client right around here actually," she says and then sips her champagne elegantly.

I nod. "That's good work."

"Not as good as writing, apparently," she says with a cheeky smile.

I hold back a chuckle. She's too adorable for me to stay sane.

"Maybe you know his nurse. You might work for the same company. He's got a live-in like you. What's her name, Liam?"

I gulp. "Millie."

Callie nearly spits out her champagne.

"What's so funny, Cal?" Nate asks.

"I'm sorry, just... old fashioned name, huh?" she says, wiping her mouth carefully as not to disturb her lipstick.

I nod. "I suppose so."

"I don't know her," Callie says sheepishly.

"It's a big city. Big world."

But if the past two months have taught me anything, it's a small city and a *very* small world.

"Right," she replies, forcing a smile.

The conversation idles only a moment, but Nate's never been able to stand silence. I think that's why he liked the rig so much. Always a constant hum of some sort of machinery in the background. Probably why he's taken so well to fatherhood as well. "Come on, guys, you don't have to act weird."

Callie and I exchange a look.

Nate sighs, holding up his hands. "We all know what happened ten years ago."

Yes. Ten years ago. That's *why we're acting weird.*

"Callie, I never told you, but I knew that you and Liam were... interested in each other or whatever," Nate says, patting his sister's hand.

"Oh?" Her surprise is weak, but it'll do. "I had no idea that you knew."

Nate eyes me. "Yeah, Liam told me." Then, he grins. "I told him he had to end things with you."

"Nate..." I say carefully. "Let's not dredge up the–"

"Not trying to dredge! Just want to get it out there. I know all of that was a long time ago, but since that's the last time you two saw each other– as far as *I* know–" He says that last part as a joke and I feel like my entrails are falling out of my body. "Well, I just want to have a nice dinner with two of my favorite people. Catch up and, yeah... " Nate goes quiet and scans the room. "I've made it weird."

Callie laughs, a tinkling little, fake laugh. "No, no, Nate. That's nice. It's good to see Liam and I hope..." Her eyes find mine. "I hope it's good to see me."

Better than good. I wake up each morning to see Callie. I ache for her until I feel her presence. If she's gone for too long, life feels sallow and empty. She's made my life so much better in the past two months than ten years of fame and fortune.

She's my everything.

And I need her to know.

"It's great to see you, Callie," I say. "As long as your brother stops making it so weird."

Callie laughs and Nate blushes. "Now, wait a second, I'm not trying to make it weird–"

"Bringing up that we had a thing is *very* weird, Nate," Callie agrees, elbowing him in the ribs.

"Okay, well, sorry, I just want us all to have a fresh start. Is that okay?"

I look at Nate and nod slowly. "More than."

⸎

Drinks and dinner go pretty smoothly after Nate has pointed out the elephant in the room. Callie and I get on just fine, stealing glances occasionally across the table. It's impossible not to look at her, the emerald vixen that I've had the privilege to have in my bed the past month.

And I have to say, I don't clean up so bad myself. I feel Callie undressing me with her eyes every so often, her gaze falling to my collarbone and to my prominent pecs tight in my shirt.

How I'd love to give her an opportunity to rip it off me.

More than that... how I'd love to have her in my arms for just one kiss, one moment with her. I need to hold her and let her know that despite Nate's presence, I still feel everything I felt before.

In fact, because he's here, I want the world to know. No more secrets, no more hiding- I want Callie to be mine.

The tattoo on the inside of her arm taunts me, reminding me of the biggest mistake of my life. It may have happened ten years ago, but hurting her, breaking her heart, that's my greatest regret.

I won't let it happen again.

"Wade also made us dessert," I say once it's clear everyone has had their fair share of the meal.

"Oh, I don't know how I could possibly –"

"Chocolate mousse cake with a raspberry coulis," I say proudly.

Nate's blue eyes grow like big puddles. "Oh no..."

"You're on vacation, Nate. Don't worry about the calories," Callie says, leaning on her elbows and giving her brother a fond smile.

"Okay. I might need a minute. And a cup of coffee." Nate glances down the hall. "And a bathroom break."

Callie laughs. "Gross."

I push myself up to standing, stabilizing myself on the table. Out of the corner of my eye, I see Callie move to get up too, but she's trying to be good, trying not to show her whole hand. "Liam, let me help you clear the table."

"No, I've got it."

"Really, it's no trouble." She jumps to her feet and starts to collect plates.

"Me too!" Nate says.

She waves him off. "You've got a bathroom to use, Nate."

Nate rolls his eyes.

"Seriously, I've got it. Give Liam and me a minute to catch up without you reminding us we kissed once or twice back in the day."

"Now, *listen*, I thought we were over that –"

"*Go!*"

I laugh to myself as Nate huffs in frustration. He follows his sister's instruction, grumbling to himself as he goes.

Alone with Callie, I'm not sure what to say to her. We clean up the table quietly and make our way to the kitchen. Only the clattering of dishes interrupts the silence... and the sound of her breath.

I want to say something. I just don't know where to start when my mind is so full of things.

"Leave the dishes," is all I can come up with. "I'll get them later."

"Are you sure?"

I nod. "Positive."

Callie goes to start the coffee. Without Nate's prying eyes, she's free to act as she has the entire time she's been here.

And so am I.

"You look amazing."

Callie stops but does not turn from the coffee maker.

"So... beautiful."

She turns around with a small smile. "So do you."

I glance down at my outfit and adjust my belt. "I look fine."

Callie is silent.

"Anyway," I say, embarrassment creeping through my veins. Maybe getting her alone wasn't such a good idea. "I'm going to get dessert ready." I open the fridge and spy the three plates covered in saran wrap that Wade set for us. They look like they belong at a Michelin restaurant: perfectly sized brown slices of mousse cake and swoops of raspberry coulis. I reach for one plate. I turn to put the plate on the island, "Wade did a really nice job, I think– "

Callie has other ideas. The moment I turn, she throws herself at me, grabbing the front of my shirt and pulling my lips to hers in a desperate kiss. The plate drops from my hand, shock overcoming my body.

I don't care about the plate, though.

All that exists is Callie.

I moan reflexively into her mouth, my bum hand sliding around her waist, the other holding onto the open fridge door for support.

"Callie, Callie, Callie, wait," I pull away from her, cradling her head in my hand.

"Mm, what? What's wrong?"

I stare down into her blinking blue eyes.

A grin creeps across her face. She pushes her thumb against the underside of my lip. "Lipstick."

My jaw hardens. I can feel the cold emanating from the fridge into my back. It's almost slowing down time. "What are we doing?"

"What do you mean?"

"This." I gesture between us. "*This*. What are we doing, Callie?"

Her eyebrows perk up. "I don't know, Liam."

Just say it, Liam.

"I..."

Tell her how you feel.

"I... love you, Callie."

I hear her breath catch in her chest. The shock is apparent on her face.

Keep going.

I pull her tighter to me. "And I want him to know."

"Want me to know what?"

Nate's voice hits me like a ton of bricks. Callie pushes me away, my back hitting the shelves of the fridge, dishes clattering inside.

"What the hell is going on, guys?"

I close the fridge and finally draw my eyes to Nate. He's standing in the doorway of the kitchen, his usual cheerful demeanor completely gone.

"Nate, it's..." Callie trails off, looking to her brother, then to me, and back again. "It's a really long story."

Nate, though, is looking squarely at me. Our eyes are locked.

I already know what this means.

"Let's have dessert and we can–" Callie takes a step between the two of us. "We can talk about it."

"No, I want him to tell me." Nate takes a few steps closer to me.

Callie rushes up to her brother, but he shrugs her off. "Nate, please don't do anything stupid!"

"What the fuck do you want to tell me, Liam?" he asks.

Remember when I said Nate was smaller, but he was stronger? Well, this is one of those moments I can feel his strength. His muscles tense under his flannel shirt. I can practically see his biceps bulge when he crosses his arms.

"Callie is my nurse, Nate," I say.

He purses his lips.

"She's been my nurse for two months." I glance at Callie and feel my breath steady. I love her. And I'm doing this for her.

For us.

"And I'm in love with her."

"Like hell you are."

I can't help but laugh. "She's not a kid anymore, Nate. She's a woman." I smile ruefully. "In fact, I should know."

I see the anger flicker through Nate's eyes before I feel his hands collide with my chest. With all his might, he pushes me backward. I stumble, trying to catch myself on the counter, but stumble back. As soon as my tailbone makes contact with the floor, I feel shooting pain up my body. All those old injuries scream at me to be careful.

"Nate, *stop*. You'll hurt him."

"Callie, stay out of this. He did this to himself," Nate growls. He steps over me and grabs me by the collar. "I told you to stay away from her."

His fist makes contact with my jaw. Powerful. Enough to bruise. I cry out and struggle beneath him. I can taste blood.

"Nate!"

"That was ten *fucking* years ago." I kick my foot against his shin. Nate loses his balance and falls to his knees. I take the opportunity to push him to the ground. To hell with my injuries. I force him to the floor, press my elbow into his chest, and fire back a punch with all my might right into his nose.

The crack of bones breaking is almost louder than his scream of pain. Blood streams out from his nose immediately. I can still feel the punch throbbing in my hand.

"You broke my nose man!" Nate pushes me off him.

I lean up against the lower cabinets, trying to catch my breath. "You punched me first."

Callie goes to Nate. "Damn, that's a lot of blood."

"No shit it's a lot of blood."

I spit out the blood in my mouth. Not as much as his, but still something.

Not enough for her to choose me.

"We have to get him to the hospital," Callie says, looking at me with ferocity. "There's too much blood."

Just like everything in my life, I've gone too far.

And at this point, I think I've lost everything.

Chapter 18

Callie

"Yep, that's a break alright."

I stare at the backlit x-ray. The break is clear, fluorescent bone interrupted with a dark black splotch.

"How are you feeling, Nathan?" the doctor, an older gentleman with a deep voice and a scraggly beard, asks with a chipper smile that no one should have this late at night.

"Like my nose is broken," Nate grumbles.

I eye my brother from my seat against the wall. He's seated on an examination table in the ER, blood still crusted under his nose and chin, holding a bag of ice to his face. But from the look in his eyes, it seems like he couldn't care less. I'm quite sure the only thing on his mind is wishing he could have clocked Liam on the nose just as hard.

Liam is currently in the waiting room. He was so good in the aftermath of Nate's injury. He called Frederick for the car, helped Nate up off the ground, and drove us to the nearest hospital. Despite me begging him to head home, he wouldn't. Of course, he wouldn't.

I can't get him out of my head. Liam just told me he loved me. And I didn't have the opportunity to say it back. Which is for the best, all things considered.

"It's pretty bad, but I think we can realign it manually."

Nate's eyes flutter shut. I bet that feels just as bad as it sounds.

"Don't worry, we'll get you all numbed up beforehand." The doctor takes the x-ray down and flashes his cheerful smile. "You just sit tight while I go get everything set, huh?" He gives us both a nod and then slips through the privacy curtain, leaving Nate and I alone for the first time since... well, since everything.

I get to my feet and approach Nate carefully. "Let me look at it."

"Callie, don't."

"I just want to see."

"You're not on duty, alright, just let him do his—" I pull on Nate's wrist, peeling the ice from his nose. He winces.

The skin is red and tender, clearly inflamed. I touch his chin, guiding his face back and forth to get a better look. "God, he really did a number on you."

Nate pushes my hand away and covers his nose with the ice again. "I've had worse."

I recoil from him and cross my arms over my chest. The life my brother has away from me is hard to understand. Life on the rig has always eluded my comprehension. Do they have fight clubs there? Is the testosterone just too much to resist all out brawls from time to time?

"Callie..." The tone of his voice is almost apologetic, pleading for my attention.

"What, Nate?" I ask, not willing to look at him.

"Why'd you go behind my back like that? Why didn't you tell me... anything?"

I feel tears in my eyes.

"It feels like the past couple months all you've been doing is lying to me. Just all the time."

I swallow. "It's complicated, Nate."

"I don't think it is."

I suddenly find the courage to shoot him a look. "Why didn't you tell me you knew what happened? That summer? Why didn't you—"

"That's not fair."

I gape at him. "How is *that* not fair?"

Nate sighs. "That's different. I was protecting you."

"And I thought I was protecting you."

"That's... no, that's not what you were doing." Nate's blue eyes harden in mine. "You were protecting yourself, Callie."

I go silent. He's right. That's all I was doing. I was trying to hide things from Nate to preserve my image, not his safety.

"You wanted to hide it all from me so you and Liam could do... whatever you wanted. And you did, apparently." He visibly cringes. Not sure if it's from physical or emotional pain. Probably both.

I dig my fingers tighter into my arm. I need something to hold onto, even if it's just me. "He loves me, Nate."

"Come on, you don't believe that, do you?"

"You don't think he could possibly love me?"

Nate huffs, "I didn't say *that*."

"So why is it so hard to believe that– "

"You've been living in his house. He pays you money to do whatever he needs and–"

I gasp. "Do *not* speak about me like he pays me for... for *that*, Nate. That's so messed up."

"You know what I mean, Callie!"

"You have no idea what has been going on between us. You have no idea–"

"No! I don't. Because *you've been lying to me.*"

I can't reply. He's right. I just don't know why he's so mad about it. It's his best friend. Shouldn't he want both of us to be happy? What's so bad about us being happy together?

"Liam is not your man, Callie. I can guarantee it."

"How?"

"Because he's *my* friend. And you've been off limits to each other since the moment I introduced you."

I purse my lips. I'm not going to cry. I'm not going to beg, no, "But Nate, I love him!" I know there's nothing I can do.

"You need to find someone your own age. Who's not... so obsessed with his career that he can't fit you into his life. The only reason he's able to give you any kind of attention is because he doesn't have a choice but to be cooped up in his house right now. I know that's hard to hear but..."

Liam is usually jetting around the world, doing research and working on his books. He's not stuck in the house where the only way to pass the time is his young and pretty nurse.

Maybe Nate's right.

"You deserve more," Nate says with a sad smile. "More than the penthouse and whatever sweet nothings he's been spewing. I know the guy pretty well. I know how he can be with women."

"You have no idea how he's been with me, Nate."

He shakes his head. "No, I don't. You're right." Then, his face hardens. "And I don't want to know, Callie."

The doctor sweeps back into the room, humming a tune, all too happy to be popping a nose back into place. "Okay, let's get started."

Nate and I don't say another word about Liam. And we don't have to. His position is clear.

There's no world in which Liam and I can be together.

And between the man who walked away from me ten years ago and my brother who has known me since birth, I know the choice I must make.

⚬

I find Liam in the waiting room working his bum hand with his good one, pushing on the inside of his palm to ignite the nerves. He doesn't notice me until I speak. "Hi."

Liam looks up and my heart breaks. He looks so tired. And the bruise is already forming on his jawline.

"Ice," I say softly, handing him a cold compress I finagled from one of the nurses.

"Oh... thank you," Liam says raggedly, a small smile twitching onto his lips.

I sit down beside him as he finds the best position for the ice on his face.

"How's he doing?" he asks.

"It's broken. Doctor is realigning it right now."

Liam chuckles, "Yeesh. That sounds rough."

"You're the one who was briefly paralyzed," I tease.

He shrugs. "Yeah, but I know what that's like. Don't know what it's like to have your nose realigned, though."

"You should write about it."

"I'll make a note of it," he says, glancing my way.

I can't look at him. My heart has already broken into a million pieces, and I know it will break into a million more as soon as I tell him we can't be together.

Liam puts his hand on the arm of his chair, palm facing upward in an invitation.

I take it. This is probably the last time I'll hold his hand or get to be intimate with him in any way. I might as well take advantage of it. "Liam..."

"I know what you're going to say."

I look to him with wide eyes. He still tries to smile, but his usually warm brown eyes are dull.

"I know what you have to do, Callie."

This makes me angry. He's trying to be soft and nice. *Understanding*. But this man just told me he *loves* me? Why can't he act like it and fight for me like he didn't all those years ago? This is his chance.

The veins under my tattoo pulse.

"It's okay."

This isn't fair. He's anticipated me breaking his heart and, somehow, we're right back where we were ten years ago. Liam's in control. He always needs to be in control. Just like he was when he asked me to go with him to Egypt. Or demanded me to type up his stories. Or refused my treatments at the beginning.

It's Liam's world. I'm just living in it.

Not anymore, though.

"He's upset. And I care for you, but he's my brother. And he always comes first."

Liam nods. "I get it. This is why things didn't work out back then. I didn't want to make you choose. Maybe because I knew what your choice would be," he muses.

I'm only half-listening to him. Because a prayer is growing louder in my head. *Fight for me, fight for me, fucking fight for me, Liam.*

"Forget what I said," he says with an embarrassed laugh. "You know, if it's easier."

"Is it easier for you?" I ask, my throat constricting.

Liam shrugs. "Maybe a little."

And just like that, he's rescinded his love for me.

How did we get here? How did everything just... fall apart?

"Okay. Fine. Well, then I think it's best if we end our working relationship, too," I say, pulling my hand from his and sticking it between my thighs so I have no impulse to reach out and touch him.

Liam nods. "I understand."

He's not going to do it, is he? I need to learn how to walk away. And this is the ultimate test. I push myself up from my chair. "You can contact the agency about ending the contract. I've been looking for a new client for a while anyway."

"A while?" An edge of anger creeps into Liam's voice.

"Yes, actually since the day I moved in." Now I'm just trying to get bonus points for hurting him. I'll regret it in the morning, but for now, it's all I can do to keep from crying. "I didn't want it to come to this. And now here we are." I throw my hands up. "Can't say I didn't try."

Liam lets out a rueful breath and licks his lower lip, unwilling to look at me. "Right."

"Right. Well. You should go. I'm going to go check on Nate," I say and back away from the place where Liam is sitting.

He raises his brown eyes up to me, darkness at the edges. Anger? Sadness? I don't know. And it's not my job to know or care anymore.

He might have anticipated the heartbreak and taken that power from me. But this time *I* get to walk away.

This time, I'm the heartbreaker.

I have to hold onto that for now.

Chapter 19

Liam

"I think you need another pair of sandals," Emma says as she rifles through the suitcase.

"No, I don't."

She looks up to where I'm sitting in the corner with annoyance. "You need a new pair. Because these–" She reaches in and grabs my leather sandals. "Will not do."

"They're comfortable. I won't be able to break in a new pair before I go."

"I'm making an executive decision." Emma drops them in the wastebasket beside the bed.

I narrow my eyes. "You know, most people wouldn't let their employees throw things away without their consent."

"And yet you do," Emma says with a smug smile.

True. I do. Emma and Wade have both been with me for a couple years now and they are truly like my family, even if they still call me Mr. Sterling. They've looked out for me in the best and worst of times. And these past two weeks have certainly been the worst of times.

After everything fell apart with Nate and Callie, I didn't know which way was up. I returned to the apartment with a sore jaw and didn't sleep for several days. Nate skipped town as soon as his nose was fixed, not bothering to even look at me as he retrieved his suitcase. I can't say I blame him. I don't have a little sister, but if I did, I'm sure I'd be just as protective.

I can't help but feel a little hurt, though. I'm his friend. Back in the day, I understood how he pushed me away from his sister. She really was just a kid, freshly eighteen and ready to explore the world.

Now, she's a grown woman. And I'm a successful man. Sure, I have my flaws. But I could take care of her. Isn't that what most people want for their beloved sisters and daughters? A man who will take care of them? Who *wants* to take care of them?

I don't blame Callie for the rejection, though the image of her walking away has haunted me every single waking moment. When I close my eyes, I can see her silhouette bathed in green, walking away from me, abandoning me.

It's for the best. She'd just be a distraction in Egypt. A distraction for the rest of my life. And I need to get back on my A-game.

"You need shoes with more arch support," Emma says. "I'll go out and find some for you to try on today." She starts to make note of it on her phone, a list of to-dos to take care of before I leave for Egypt in just a few days. "Also, I have a few interviews set up with the agency for caregivers. Those will have to be done today if you're going to–'

"Emma, I told you. I don't need a nurse to go with me."

She raises an eyebrow. "So you were asking Callie to go with you because…?"

Emma and Wade have been suspicious of me ever since Callie left. They were both stunned, understandably. And I, being stricken by grief, didn't really have the most creative excuse. One would think because I write stories for a living, I might be better at this, but I save all of that for the page. When it comes to my real life, I flounder at lies and untruths. So, I told them that we agreed that her work with me was done. I know my exercises; I have my cane. That should be enough.

Unfortunately, they have not been very convinced by that.

"Thought I'd be in worse shape than I am," I say simply.

"When are you going to quit it with that?"

I snort, pushing myself up from the chair in the corner I've been sitting in while she goes through my packing list. "Quit it with what?"

"We both know something was going on," Emma replies.

I frown. "Excuse me?"

"With Callie."

I shake my head and limp out of the room on my cane. "You've got it all wrong."

"I don't think I do," Emma continues, following at my heels.

I love Emma, but she can be a pain in my ass.

"There was tension from day one with the two of you. You two were always laughing and giggling to each other. And don't think I didn't catch her sneaking out of your room once or twice in the middle of the day."

"What?!" I cry out, spinning on my heels. "You saw her?"

Emma smiles slyly. "Aha... I knew it."

I flush. "That doesn't prove anything."

"Are you kidding? You're as red as a beet because I *caught you*."

I start to protest, but Emma holds up her hand to stop me.

"Listen, I'm not trying to give you a hard time. I just don't want you to be muscling through this if there was something there and things didn't work out."

I consider Emma carefully. She's an earnest person. I've always liked that about her. Between all her quippy jokes and eyebrow waggles, she's a good woman. And she's always, *always* wanted the best for me. "I... it was rash. Inappropriate. She was working for me. And that became too much. It wasn't fair to her."

"Oh, bullshit, Sterling. You're not giving me the whole truth and you know it."

I stare at her, unwilling to reveal more. The story is too complicated and layered. I can't go into a flashback right this second.

"I'm just saying, it's hard for a girl to refuse a man *needing* her. You know?"

If only it were that easy. But Callie has a keeper. And while I've lamented her loss, I've lamented Nate's too.

Then it hits me.

If I want Callie, I need to go through Nate. I have to do it the way I've never been willing to.

The right way.

"Emma, I need you to get me a flight to Houston."

"Houston?" she asks, her mouth cocked in confusion.

"ASAP. *Today*. And pack me an overnight bag. There's something I need to do."

———◈———

The rig is just as I remember it. Crowded. Loud. Smelling like the salt of ocean and sweat.

I adjust my yellow hard hat as I take in the view. The ocean can be beautiful. But it can also feel like nothingness. Miles and miles of blue and waves can make a man feel stuck.

"Missed it?"

I smile at Bob, the tool pusher. He's been in charge since before I got to the rig and is closing in on retirement. "Not so much."

He lets out a loud guffaw and pats me on the back. "Come on, I'll take you to Nate."

Bob leads me into the bowels of the rig. From the outside, the thing looks like a Lovecraftian skeleton, but once you go down to the second deck, it's just the engine rooms, the galley, and living quarters.

"Thanks for giving me clearance on such short notice, Bob."

"No problem," the older man smiles. "It's always a pleasure to get a visit from one of my old hands."

I bristle at the word old.

"Couldn't get enough of Nate, huh?"

I cock an eyebrow.

"He mentioned he was going to visit you on his two weeks. Haven't heard much about the visit since he's gotten back onboard though."

I try to laugh it off. "Oh, you know. What happens in New York stays in New York."

"Is that the saying now? Well."

Bob leads me through the familiar halls of the second deck all the way to the lead engineer's office. Nate's really come up from the old days of us kicking around this place.

Bob opens the door and pokes his head inside. I wait at his elbow, trying to stay out of view. "Knock, knock. You gotta a minute, Emerson?"

"What's up?"

"Visitor for you."

I hear Nate hesitate. "A visitor?"

Bob opens the door wider for the grand reveal. "Hey, Nate."

Nate's face immediately falls.

"Don't look so happy to see me," I say with a chuckle.

Bob looks between the two of us, eyebrows raised in alarm. "What happens in New York, I guess. Well, I'll leave you two for a minute."

"No need, Bob. You can see him out. I won't be needing to talk with him," Nate says, returning his gaze to the computer in front of him.

"Would you cut that out and give me just five minutes to talk to you like a man instead of running away from me?" I ask aggressively. I didn't fly all the way out here for him to say fuck off.

Bob puts his hand on my arm. "Easy, kid. "

Nate narrows his eyes at me. "Five minutes."

I shake off Bob's grip and give him a polite, if awkward, smile as I step into the office. The heavy door shuts behind me, leaving Nate and I alone in the tiny office. I size him up as if we're about to fight again: he's clad in a bright orange jumpsuit, the usual apparel for guys on duty, and wears a pair of reading glasses for the computer. "Nose looks good."

"Shut the hell up."

"Okay, we're off to a good start."

Nate's gaze lazes away from me to the computer. "What do you want, Kaminsky?"

"Can I sit?"

"You do whatever you want anyway, so who am I to stop you?"

I roll my eyes and sit in the rickety rolling chair beside Nate's. The computer is full of diagrams and numbers I don't understand anymore. Don't know if I ever did. I've always been better with words, if I'm honest. "You didn't give me a chance to talk to you before you left."

"Your actions said everything."

I nod. "That's fair. So do yours."

Nate shoots me a scathing look. "What was I supposed to do? I found out my sister and best friend were lying to me for months. And all the while they'd been..." he trails off and shakes his head. "Ten years ago, I told you that you and Callie could never happen. *Never.* Then I come to find out–"

"She was a kid then, Nate. She's not a kid anymore."

"Don't you think I know that?! It plagues me every day to know my little sister is out there in the world just being ogled and looked at and used up."

"I didn't use her."

"Sure, Liam."

"I didn't. Both Callie and I were shocked when she was assigned to work with me."

Nate picks up a pen from the desk and starts clicking it over and over again. "Then why didn't you say anything?"

"Because we both knew how you felt about us being around each other! We didn't want to make things weird or–"

"You made things weird! You didn't say anything and it–"

"We liked being around each other, Nate! What more can I say?"

His furrowed brow relaxes slightly.

"Look, I know that you never wanted us together. But we were. Ten years ago, those two months I was with Callie, I..." *Say it. You're not a coward anymore.* "I fell in love with her. And I didn't even know it. You told me no and I told myself I was kidding myself. Caught up in the summer heat and gorgeous sunsets and–" I stop short and fold my hands between my knees. Like I'm praying. "Seeing her again brought all that back. I tried to avoid it, but I couldn't." I meet Nate's gaze.

Those blue eyes, nearly identical to Callie's. The closest I've come to looking into her eyes in weeks. "I couldn't. I wasn't strong enough."

Nate's anger has completely faded. It almost looks like he's... afraid.

"I love her. I do. She's funny and smart and doesn't take my shit. She holds me accountable. She listens." I could keep listing things I love about her. The way she looks in her scrubs, the blonde hairs she leaves behind in my bed, the way her hand fits around my ribs. The ink on the inside of her arm. The connection she's kept to me all these years. "Nate, you need to know what an honor it would be to love and be loved by your sister."

Nate lets out a tight breath as if the wind has been knocked out of him. His eyes are slightly glazed. "Damn, man."

I chuckle. "Sorry."

"No, that was... no wonder you're a writer."

"Now, listen, I don't just have sweet words to say, I mean it. I'm just a man, Nate. A man in love."

"I know. I know you're not just talk." He twiddles his fingers and then knocks his fist against the desk. "Fuck."

I think I've done it. Wedged myself into the small crack in his façade.

"You're just reminding me of how I felt with Felicity. You know?" Nate takes a deep breath to keep his eyes from watering any further. "How big that feeling is when it's right."

I smile softly. "I'm glad you can understand where I'm coming from."

Nate pinches the bridge of his nose and shakes his head.

"Listen, I'm your friend, Nate. I'd never want to hurt you. And I'd never, ever want to hurt Callie."

He considers this for a moment and then drops his eyes into his lap. "I've thought for a long time that you being with her would hurt me. You'd pull her away from me. You'd draw away from me, more than you already do."

"We're getting older and we have responsibilities."

"I know. But that doesn't mean I don't miss you, man."

My heart swells. I haven't been a good friend the past ten years. It doesn't mean I don't think about him often or want the absolute best for him. "I'm sorry I haven't been the friend I should have been all these years. I'm ready to... do better. For everyone."

Nate tries to hold back a smile, but it doesn't work.

"I flew all the way out here and took a boat from the mainland to this godforsaken place, didn't I?"

He chuckles. "Look, I'm still not sure about all this. You and Callie. But if you mean what you say..." Nate nods hard. "Then go for it."

I can't believe my ears. "Seriously?"

"I guess so," Nate says with a lopsided smile.

"You won't regret it. I promise." I hold my hand out for him to shake it. In classic Nate fashion, he takes it and pulls me in for a hug.

"If you hurt her, I'll castrate you," he murmurs in my ear.

I laugh, but I know he means it. "Who knows? She might hurt me."

"As she should."

We break apart. "Would you put in a good word for me?"

"Eh, if she asks me to. But you've got to do this one on your own," Nate says. "That's the first test."

I nod. That's fair. I have to prove I'm man enough to admit the mistakes of the past.

"After all. You love her. Right?"

Without hesitation, I answer: "Yes. More than anything."

More than anything I've ever known.

Chapter 20

Callie

Mindy Parker is an easy client. She gets up at seven a.m. on the dot and is in bed shortly before eight. She takes the same meals, three times a day, and has no problems swallowing pills. She does not argue with me about doing her exercises and is generally pleasant to be around.

And yet, these past two weeks, I've never been more miserable.

I should feel lucky that the agency already had a new client waiting for me when I called the morning I left Liam's for good. I should be happy.

But I'm not.

I don't know how it's possible I reached a new low. For ten years, I've lived with Liam leaving me as my rock bottom.

I would never have thought in a million years that me leaving *him* would feel worse.

Worse than worse.

While Mindy Parker will certainly be the easiest money I will ever make, I miss the volatility of Liam and his schedule. I miss his demands, his complaints, his wry comments.

And of course, I miss his body. I miss being utterly consumed in his arms, held tight to his chest, wishing our bodies would slowly meld together until they are one.

Even if we can never become the same body, I can't help the feeling that I am still attached to him. And now, I've been horribly, violently separated.

"Callie, dear," Mindy calls out for me from her settee.

"Yes, Mindy?" I answer from where I stand in the kitchen.

"A cup of tea, if you wouldn't mind."

"Of course."

Mindy does not have other staff. It is just me and her. She lives in a townhouse on the Upper West Side and, while she doesn't have a view of Central Park, it's rather lavish. This is where she and her husband lived since they were young, where her children grew up, where she now resides alone with a purebred Persian cat named Gracie. Her husband passed many years ago from a heart attack and whenever she brings him up, she whispers, "God rest his soul," right afterward.

I set to making Mindy's cup of tea. She is, as I have said, a simple woman, and only requires me to boil water in a kettle on the stove so she can dunk her Twining's tea bag in it. There are boxes of unopened, fancier tea brands in the cabinet that one of her daughters buys for her when she travels. She can't bring herself to touch them.

Kettle on the stove, I step back and lean against the opposite counter of the small galley kitchen, watching. For what, I don't know. Something to change, perhaps. What if the kettle exploded suddenly, leaving my face mangled and maimed? It'd be terrible, but at least it'd be different.

Then I'd have something else to think about rather than Liam Kaminsky.

Ever since that day two and a half weeks ago that I walked away from him, my arm has ached. I can't explain it. There's no reason that it should ache. Other than some weird cosmic retribution. I want to pluck each of these daisies off my arm and destroy them in my hands once more.

But these daisies are permanent. That was the point, wasn't it?

After I told Liam of the meaning, he couldn't stop looking at my tattoo. At first it made me uncomfortable until I realized he was repenting in some way for the pain he'd caused me. As he traced the lines of ink, it was as if he was reliving the moment he left me again and again.

What I wouldn't give to hear him whisper in my ear again... something, anything.

He told me he loved me.

God, I should have said it back. That's my biggest regret. Not saying it back when I had a chance. Maybe then it wouldn't have been so easy for us to walk away from one another.

Now, here I am, watching a kettle and waiting for it to boil.

Story of my life.

Stop thinking about him, Cal.

I can't stop.

He's not worth it.

That's not true. It's not that he's not worth it. It's that I can't have him.

This is the right thing to do.

But how can it be when my whole body aches for him? My arm isn't the only thing.

In the dark hours in my new room at Mindy Parker's, I imagine Liam in bed with me. He'd probably complain that he's a little too tall for the bed and I'd giggle into his chest. We'd lay there in an embrace, quiet as mice, knowing that Mindy was on the other side of the wall, not wanting to interrupt her sleep.

But knowing Liam, we just wouldn't be able to help ourselves. He would start rocking into me and I would half-heartedly admonish him.

Half-heartedly.

Because I'd want whatever he wanted to give me.

Slowly but surely, we would tangle together, our kisses growing more and more intense until it just becomes too much to bear. He'd push his hand into my waistband, dip his fingers into me and–

"You're wet," he'd say with a grin, right into my ear.

His voice is still so potent in my memory.

Sometimes, it's almost as if I can feel the stubble of his face scratching against my cheek... against the inside of my thighs.

I'd be too impatient for that, though. I'd force his pants down and slip him between my legs. I'd let him know what I wanted.

And I know he'd oblige. Enthusiastically.

With someone on the other side of the wall, he'd save his grunts and moans for me. Quiet, rumbling in his gut. I'd feel every one as we descend into pleasure.

Suddenly, the kettle whistles, loud and proud.

Snap the hell out of it, Callie.

I snatch the kettle off the burner and pour the water into a teacup for Mindy. As I bring it over to her with a sachet of raspberry tea, I feel how wet I've gone between my legs. Just thinking about Liam makes me wet.

I need to stop thinking about him during the workday. It's really throwing off my groove. I need to save the imaginings for late at night when I can slip my hand under the sheets and do something about my arousal.

"Mmm, thank you, Callie dear," Mindy says with a smile.

I wonder if she can tell I'm miserable. A little old lady doesn't deserve a miserable live-in nurse during the final years of her life.

"Sit with me and watch my program, would you?"

I force a smile. "Of course." I take a seat in one of the chairs. It creaks under my weight and is most uncomfortable, but it's the least I can do for Mindy.

Mindy exclusively watches BBC America and right now, episodes of *As Time Goes By* are playing seemingly ad infinitum, a show featuring her beloved Dame Judy Dench. I stare at the screen unsure of what's happening, but to be sitting here with Mindy while she sips her tea contentedly is quite enough for me.

I feel my phone buzz in the pocket of my scrubs. I glance at Mindy. I don't usually like having my phone out, but she's never seemed to have a problem with it.

When I take it out, I can't keep my jaw from dropping.

Liam's name appears on the screen. And with it, a message.

Callie...

The preview stops there. I have to open the app to see the rest. He's written something that looks like a letter. That's very Liam. Very Liam indeed.

Callie,

I'm flying to Cairo tomorrow. I want you to come with me. Plane departs from Teterboro at noon. Don't worry about what you pack, we will get you everything you need.

Please. I need you by my side.

XXX

Those three goddamn x's. They make my heart flutter with anticipation.

"What are you smiling about?"

I glance over at Mindy. She's got a sneaky smile on her face. "Huh?"

"I may be old, but I know your whole life is in that thing," she says, pointing a crooked finger at that phone. "And I know there are only two reasons you'd be smiling at that godforsaken box like that. You've either received a surprising windfall of cash to your bank account or..."

I giggle.

Mindy leans toward me and whispers knowingly, "It's a boy."

I bite my lower lip and nod. "Something like that."

She settles back into her seat, returning her gaze to the television, triumphant.

Little does she know, this is so much more complicated than a boy. It's a man. A man I've known for so many years and have lost before.

I'm so close to losing him again. I don't know if my soul can bear it.

But sitting here with Mindy... I've worked so hard to get here. My dream career. My dream city.

Can I just give that all up for a man? Would I be giving anything up at all?

Not to mention there's one thing standing in the way of all of this.

My brother.

———◆◇◆———

I've been calling Nate nonstop since Mindy went to bed. He's not picking up. I've thought about the time difference. Maybe he's still on shift. Or maybe his satellite phone is out of juice. That always happens when he's out there on the rig.

Or maybe he's ignoring me. We haven't spoken much since he left New York. He was out of here like a flash. There have been occasional texts and check-ins but zero discussion of Liam.

I'm not giving up though. All I can do is pace back and forth, back and forth. I wouldn't be surprised if I wore a hole in the carpet from how much I'm pacing, praying he'll pick up.

Finally, after the umpteenth phone call, I hear Nate's voice.

"Well, *someone* wants my attention."

"Thank God you picked up; I need to talk to you."

"Is this about... "

"Liam. Yes. I know you probably don't want to talk about it but–"

"What's going on, Callie?"

I swallow. Time to spill my guts. "Liam wants me to go to Cairo with him tomorrow and I want to say yes." I smack my hand across my mouth, surprised I just vomited that all out.

To my shock, my brother chuckles. *Chuckles.* What's going on? "And?"

"Why are you so calm?" I ask.

"It's your life, Cal. You can make your own choices."

I stop pacing and stare at the blue striped, floral wallpaper. "That's not what you were saying two weeks ago."

Nate sighs, "I know. I'm sorry about that. It's your life... what you do is totally up to you."

"Even with Liam?"

"Even with Liam. As much as it pains me to say it."

My heart feels so light and yet leaden at the same time. "Wow. Um. When did you change your mind?"

"Change of heart, I guess."

"Wow, ten years and a change of heart happens in two weeks," I say dryly.

"You want me to change it back?"

I collapse onto the bed and grab one of the pillows, hugging it to my chest with a giddy smile. "No."

"Fine. I won't." Nate pauses. "So, you want to go with him."

I groan, "I don't know."

"Why? It's an all-expense paid trip to Egypt!"

"That's not... "

"With the man you– I can't believe I'm saying this– love! Or like! Or whatever."

The word love feels so big and terrifying.

Probably because it's true.

"I mean do you like him? Or love him? Or some other word I don't know?"

I know my answer. But saying it out loud to someone else is new for me. "Yeah. I do. I love him, Nate."

"Then you're going."

"But my job–"

"You won't need one if you're with Liam. Have you seen that guy's net worth?"

I click my tongue in annoyance. "That's not the point and you know it."

"I know, I'm just giving you a hard time."

"I've worked really hard to get where I am. I've wanted this for a long time. Who am I if I just run away to Cairo for a man?"

Nate takes a deep breath. "Can you hear me okay?"

"Yes."

"I want you to hear every word."

Jeez, he sounds serious. "I'm listening, Nate."

"Yes, you've worked really hard. And we're all so proud of you, Callie. And I know you're proud of yourself too. That's the most important thing. In my experience, though, jobs are a dime a dozen. People aren't."

I feel my heart tighten. He's right.

"When I was dating Felicity, I knew that was it. And I know that will always be it. If I'd had to have sacrificed my job to be with her, I would have. Because I knew. Do you know, Callie?"

Do I know beyond a shadow of a doubt Liam is the one? The man I spent a month with when I was eighteen and two more months with ten years later?

Someone who has spent most of my life as a stranger? Yet feels like an implicit part of me?

"Figure out if you know. Because that's your answer."

Chapter 21

Liam

My whisky is now muddled with water, the ice cubes half melted. I haven't been able to take a sip. Since Andie, the flight attendant, poured me the drink, all I've been doing is staring into the amber liquid. Waiting.

The door to the cockpit opens and the pilot emerges. Rodrigo has flown me many times all around the world. He manages to make even the worst turbulence feel like floating on air. "Mr. Sterling, it's been 30 minutes."

I glance at my watch. He's right. It's going on twelve thirty. We were supposed to take off at noon, but I demanded we hold the plane.

Callie will come.

At least I really thought she would.

"We cannot hold much longer, what with the fuel and the air traffic," Rodrigo says carefully.

"Just ten more. Then we'll go."

Rodrigo forces a polite smile. "Very well, sir." Then, he disappears back into the cockpit.

I glance out my window at the tarmac. Empty except for a man in a yellow vest meandering around. "Come on, Callie..."

I should have done more. I knew I should have done more. Should have called the agency and figured out where she was working now. But that would have been creepy. But is a text enough? It certainly lacks romance. It's not exactly the sweeping gesture I want it to be.

I close my eyes. I need to prepare myself in the event she doesn't come. Thirty minutes late to our take-off time is a message, isn't it?

Maybe she's given up on me. I can't blame her, but my heart breaks.

I love her.

And I've loved her a long time.

———◄◦►———

Ten years earlier...

The frogs out here are loud. They are unfettered by fear and call to each other with abandon.

Callie and I sit side by side at the end of an unleveled dock. Why a pond this size needs a dock, I'm not sure. I can't imagine anyone fishing here. All they'd come up with would be a hook full of algae.

But it's a perfect place to sit on a summer night and enjoy the moon.

There is a respectful distance between Callie and I. While we've been at this clandestine fling a little more than a week and a half, it's still new. We're still basically strangers. During the day, we don't really have time to get to know each other.

Dinnertime is always the most nerve-wracking time for me at the Emerson household. Mr. and Mrs. Emerson are friendly, the type of parents who ask lots of questions, disregarding if they're too invasive or not. But ever since Callie and I kissed, I feel like everyone can see it on my face. One wrong move, one slip of the tongue, and dinner will turn into a trial.

Callie and I have sat across from each other at every dinner since I've arrived. And while we don't usually converse one on one, it's given me plenty of time to study her. I've watched her skin tan and freckles appear as summer deepens. I've noticed the way she looks when she's bored, her eyes rolling around the room, trying to find something to keep her entertained.

And it's here where we first locked eyes and my whole body caught on fire.

They're right when they say blue is the hottest part of the flame. Her eyes have shown me that.

Tonight, my body has been on fire for hours, waiting for the house to be quiet so we can find the right time to sneak out.

It's nearly midnight as we sit here on the dock. And yet I don't feel tired at all. I'm too excited.

Callie just does this to me.

"Do you think you'll stay on the rig for the rest of your life?" she asks out of the blue, cutting through the croaking frogs.

I laugh. "That's a big question."

She flushes and shrugs.

"Not a bad question. Just a big one." I look at her out of the corner of my eye. She's feeling shy. I've got to draw her out. "Why do you ask?"

Callie tucks some hair behind her hair. "Nate loves it."

I nod. "That's true."

"Which, I don't get. Like why would you want to be stuck in the middle of the ocean for two weeks at a time to... I don't even know what you guys do."

"Me either, most of the time."

She giggles, a big smile on her face.

I shift myself closer to her. Just a little bit. "This okay?"

Callie shifts too. Her shoulder brushes against mine. "Yeah. Definitely."

We exchange a smile. I'm a grown man and yet I feel butterflies in my stomach. No woman has made me feel like this since I was thirteen, nursing a horrible celebrity crush on Scarlett Johansson. I look back at the pond, glowing only in the moonlight. "I really hope I'm not there the rest of my life. It was fun at first, but now... I feel stuck."

Callie touches my forearm, caressing it tentatively. "What would you do if you could do anything?"

"It's not as simple as that."

"It's just a question."

I sigh. "I... I can't say."

Callie shakes my arm. "Why?"

"Because it's embarrassing."

"Now you *have* to tell me."

I shake my head. "Nope."

"*Liaaaaaam*. You have to! Or else I'll guess."

"Not telling."

Callie pauses, lips twisting in thought. "You want to be a rodeo clown, don't you?"

I laugh. "What?! No!"

"It's okay, Liam. The first step to recovery is *admitting* it."

"I don't want to be a- "

"I think you'd make a very good rodeo clown."

I scoff, "Why do you say that?"

"Big feet," she says with a nod at my shoes.

"Have you been staring at my feet, Callie?" I tease.

Even in the dark, I can see her blush. "Not on purpose."

"Do you have a foot thing or— "

"Everyone always says if someone has big feet, they'll have a big dick! I can't help but be curious."

We both go silent. I'm the first to break though, an amused laugh spilling out of me.

"I'm not saying I'm thinking about your dick, but—"

"I think you *did* just say you're thinking about my dick." I smile smugly. "It's okay. I'm flattered, really."

Callie sighs. "Well, don't get any ideas."

I consider her tenderly. I know she's a virgin. She made that abundantly clear after I first kissed her. "Don't get any ideas, Liam Kaminsky. I'm not sleeping with you."

It didn't bother me at all. I'd had my wild days where all I wanted was sex, no strings attached. I'm not sure if I'm ready for more or if Callie brings something out of me.

Probably a little of both.

"Come here," I had whispered, wrapping my hand around her hip and pulling her to my chest. I kissed the crown of her head and feel her body relax into mine. Her hand rested on my belly. "No ideas, I promise."

Now, Callie tilts her head back. "I'm still not done trying to figure out what you actually want to do with your life."

"Ugh… I know you're not." I look up at the sky, take in the darkness, the stars, the moon. "I've never said it out loud to someone."

"You can trust me."

"I know I can, Callie." I squeeze her tighter. "That's what scares me." Three weeks at the Emerson house and I'm completely captivated by her. "Promise you won't laugh?"

"Never."

I've taken bigger risks in my life. Kissing her in the hallway of her childhood home while her brother was hogging the bathroom was one of those. And yet, this moment feels bigger than that. "I write things. That's my hobby. You know, to unwind on the rig. And I think I'm kinda good at it. I think I'd like to do that."

Callie is quiet. I'm afraid she's about to laugh at me. It's a frivolous dream. That's what my dad would have told me. "Liam."

I look down at her. In her eyes is… adoration and maybe even love.

"I think you'd make a great writer."

And that's when I know. All these feelings bubbling in my chest for her don't come from lust or immediate gratification.

They come from love.

It feels uncalculated and rash but screw it.

I love her.

I can't tell her that, though. So instead, I kiss her deep and hard on the mouth. Maybe she'll feel it.

Present Day

The barren landscape of the tarmac is interrupted by a golfcart whizzing toward the plane.

No. It couldn't be.

My heart starts to pound as the cart grows closer.

It skids to a stop right by the stairs that I've demanded to be left outside the plane. The driver leaps off and collects a suitcase from the back and from the passenger seat...

It's her.

Callie Emerson in the flesh.

She steps off the cart and looks up at the plane, her blue-eyed wonder filling me with ecstasy.

I leap up from my seat, cane in hand, and go to the cabin door, which has been sealed. "Open this, Andie," I demand, my voice trembling with anxiety.

Andie hurries to meet me. "Right away, sir."

As I watch her, I realize how tyrannical I sounded. "Please. Sorry. Please open this..."

The seal breaks, the door slides open, and I'm hit with a cool New Jersey wind. I step out onto the stairs and there she is. Callie is at the base of the stairs, looking up at me. Her awe turns into a grand smile.

"You made it," I say so softly I feel like the wind has carried my voice away.

"You held the plane!" she cries out.

"Of course, I did."

Callie carefully begins to climb the stairs, one by one, until she can't take the anticipation anymore. She runs up the last few and throws her arms around me, pulling me into a deep, unflinching kiss. "Thank you," she whispers when she pulls away.

My good hand holds tight to her waist while my bad one tenderly strokes the side of her face. Callie pushes her cheek into my hand, eyes fluttering shut.

"You... you're coming with me?" I ask.

"Yes."

"To Cairo?"

"Wherever you want to go, I'm coming with you. And I'm so sorry I'm late. The traffic was horrendous. And, once again, my phone died."

I've never been filled with so much happiness. "You talked to Nate."

"He gave his blessing."

"Your job."

She shrugs, laughter on her lips, "Screw it." Her cerulean eyes glimmer in mine. "There are a million jobs. There's only one you, Liam."

"Damn, that's good. I should use it in a book."

"Just add me to the acknowledgments."

"You deserve at least a dedication," I say, holding her tighter. "Every dedication." I kiss her forehead. "For the rest of my life."

Callie giggles and then runs her hands up my chest. "Liam, I love you."

It hits me like a ton of bricks. The most welcome collision of my life. "You know I love you, Callie."

"Mr. Sterling–" Rodrigo's voice comes from inside the plane. "We really do need to–"

"Yes!" I say, snapping out of my trance. "Yes, of course. We are ready when you are."

I usher her onto the plane and situate us both in our seats. Callie's arm loops through mine. "That's nice," I murmur.

"Get used to it, I'm never letting go."

"I wouldn't want it any other way."

Andie closes the cabin door. The plane begins to taxi, readying for takeoff.

"It's a long flight," I say to her.

"I know."

"And Cairo will be hot."

Callie smirks. "I'm aware."

"And we've got a schedule to keep."

"That's just fine." She slides her hand into my injured one. With just a simple touch from Callie, I feel stronger. "I'll never be more than a step behind."

I never knew that love was meant to feel like this. It makes me more courageous. But that's just what Callie's love does.

Together, I think our love could conquer the world.

Chapter 22

Epilogue

*O*ne year later...

"*The streets of Tokyo were suspiciously quiet that night. Gregory could feel dread creeping up his spine as he walked his usual route to the Persimmon Club...*" Liam recites as I type furiously at the laptop.

We've just returned from Japan, our third trip in the past year. First Egypt, then New Zealand, then Japan. Each for research for Liam's latest series of books. Man, have we had adventures. The first book was published soon after we delivered the manuscript and has been received to wide acclaim. Detective Gregory Oaks has become a feature of the Zeitgeist and HBO has already been in contact for the rights.

Liam is like a machine when it comes to his writing. He's somehow able to churn out books in weeks flat.

Of course, he has a great assistant.

More than a year out from his accident, Liam is mostly recovered. He walks without a cane and is able to enjoy most activities that he did before the accident. However, his right hand still isn't quite up to speed when it comes to typing and so, I play the happy typist.

I've come to love the job. I love being a part of Liam's process, aiding in the creation of his wild and winding stories. I can't imagine most people are this close to the art of the person they love. But me? Well, I guess I'm lucky.

"*When Gregory reached the club, it was the same old song and dance,*" Liam goes on. "*'What's the password?' the decrepit doorman asked, his missing front tooth whistling as he spoke.*"

I stop and frown at the document. "His tooth whistled?"

Liam looks up from his easy armchair. "His missing tooth whistled."

"But the missing tooth didn't whistle. The space where his tooth once was whistled."

Liam rolls his eyes. "Semantics, Callie. We can clean it up in editing."

"I'm just saying, it's confusing. It doesn't make sense. Why wait if we can do it now?"

He grumbles something to himself and then folds his hands to his mouth in a prayer position. He's thinking. "*...words accompanied by a whistling due to his missing front tooth.*"

"Better," I reply.

"Well, thanks."

I eye him over the laptop screen and catch him smirking at me. "What's that face?"

Liam shakes his head slowly. "No face. Just smiling at you."

I feel my chest flush. Still after a year together, he manages to get my pulse racing. That little quirk of his lips is his tell. He's thinking about me and probably my body. He's thinking of all the things he'd like to do to me. "Need I remind you that we have five chapters due tomorrow and we're only on–"

"Chapter three. I know. You don't need to remind me."

"Then why are you looking at me like that?"

"Aren't I allowed to undress my girlfriend with my eyes every now and then? Is that a crime?" he asks, pushing his hair out of his eyes.

My stomach flips. Yes, he's more than allowed. He's welcome to. "You can't say things like that and not expect me to... you know..."

"Not expect you to what?" he asks with a playful smile.

"You're flustering me, Liam!"

Liam chuckles. "Perfect. That's how I like it."

My phone buzzing in my pocket interrupts our conversation. Thank God or else I might just have to abandon our work altogether, leap onto his lap, and tear his clothes off. I whip it out from my pocket. "Sorry, it's a client."

"By all means. We're due for a break anyway."

I answer the phone and head toward the library. "Hey Bethany! How're you feeling?'

"Back is aching. Knees are aching. Everything is aching."

I chuckle. My client, Bethany, has just had twins and is recovering from a c-section. I'm part of her postpartum care team and it's been such a pleasure helping her navigate this part of her journey. And it helps that her twins are the most adorable newborns I've ever seen. "You want to go over a schedule for this next week?"

"*Please.*"

Since returning to the states after our trip to Cairo, I've become a visiting nurse. No live-in positions anymore, especially now that I live with Liam so there is no need for that sort of thing. And this way, I can take on clients for a month or two between trips with Liam.

I have to admit, the flexibility I get from Liam's money is *divine.* However, I didn't want to abandon all the work I'd done to become a nurse in the first place. Helping people still gives me that rush. Liam has been nothing but supportive of my goals.

After I finish up on the phone, I return to the living room where Liam is now pacing near my workstation. He's got a pensive look on his face.

"Okay, where were we?" I say with a chipper smile. I plop down in my chair.

"Read me a lead in, would you?" Liam asks.

"Uh... okay." I scan the page for a good starting point. "*Gregory... song and dance.* Okay, here. *'What's the password?' the decrepit doorman asked, his missing front tooth whistling as he* – oh, we're changing that, aren't we? What was it you said?"

Liam blinks. "I don't –"

"Oh, I got it!" I say triumphantly. "...*words accompanied by a whistling due to his missing front tooth*. Okay, backing up."

"Callie..."

"Sorry, we're about to get right back into it, I swear. *'What's the password?' the decrepit doorman asked, words accompanied by a whistling due to his missing front tooth.* Then Gregory replies, '*Will you marry me?*'" Huh? "I didn't write that, did I?" I start to hit the backspace button.

I feel Liam's hand on my wrist. "Maybe I need to be more direct."

I freeze. More direct? I look up at him with wide eyes. "What do you..."

Liam smiles gently and then sinks down to one knee.

I gape at him. "Liam..."

"I thought it'd be clever, but maybe I misjudged," he says, reaching into his pocket and producing a small velvet box.

"Oh my God."

"Callie..."

"You're really doing this."

"Would you pull up your sleeve?"

I frown. That's a strange way to begin a proposal.

"I promise, there's a point," he says with a lopsided smile. He nods toward my left sleeve. "Please."

I fulfill his request, rolling my sleeve up, revealing my tattoo.

"Daisies are a symbol for many things. When I gave them you all those years ago, I wanted them to be a symbol of my affection for you, even if I couldn't keep you." Liam took a deep breath. "But in the language of flowers, they mean much more. Innocence... purity... perhaps that's what they were back then. A testament to your spirit which I was too afraid to taint."

Liam swallows. "There is another meaning of daisies in the language of flowers, though." He stops short.

"What's that, Liam?"

He smiles. "New beginnings."

I glance down at the tattoo. Inked out of spite at first, embraced by my need to move on, and now... the meaning has transformed again.

"I've loved you for many years. You've changed my life a million times over with your courage and your compassion. And I want to spend the rest of my life with you."

I've never smiled so hard in my life.

"Our life will be full of daisies. New beginnings. Over and over. Adventures to new places, new jobs, new books. Maybe even more." His eyes sparkle. I can see it, a future for us. A family.

"But I want to start it with this one." Liam opens the box. The ring inside sparkles brilliantly. "Callie.... *Callista...*"

"Not my full name..." I groan with a laugh.

"I'm sorry, I know you hate that," Liam says with a chuckle. Another breath. And then, in the most earnest way, he asks, "Will you marry me?"

I find myself nodding before I can muster words. "Y-yes. Yes, of course. I... yes, I'll marry you," I say, my voice wavering with emotion.

Liam takes my hand in his and slips the ring onto my finger. "Perfect fit," he says with a sigh of relief.

The cool metal around my finger feels strange, but so right. Our love has been eleven years in the making. And while I would have been happy to continue my relationship with Liam, married or not, knowing I'll be his for the rest of our lives fills me with joy.

I throw my arms around his neck, collapsing into him. He gasps at the force of my body against his. I bury my face into his neck, descending into tears.

"Happy tears, Cal?"

I look at him, tears pouring from my eyes, smile on my lips. "The happiest."

Liam smiles and kisses me tenderly on the lips. "I love you."

"I love you. So much." I stroke the stubble on his cheeks, feeling the warmth of his eyes wrap around me. This is the man of my dreams. I can't believe how lucky I am.

And now that he's here in my arms, now that we're engaged, well, there's only one way to celebrate.

I kiss him passionately, pushing my body up against his as tight as possible, making it known I want him.

"Callie…"

"I love you, Liam."

"My God, I love you."

"Let me show you how much," I say, running my fingers through his hair.

There's a heavy knock at the door. *Shit.* We just keep getting interrupted.

I jerk my head to look in that direction. "Who is that?"

"I don't know," Liam says through a tight breath. From the bulge in his crotch, I know he's just as disappointed by the interruption as I am. "Why don't you check, and I can sort myself out?"

I narrow my eyes at Liam. From the look on his face, he knows the answer. He's just not willing to tell me. "Wade and Emma won't be in until tomorrow."

"True."

"And Frederick knows not to send people up without clearance."

"Of course."

My curiosity is overwhelming. I get to my feet even though leaving Liam's embrace is *painful*. As I go to the front door, I twist the ring on my finger. It doesn't feel real. I'm engaged to Liam Kaminsky. My first and last love.

It doesn't get better than this.

When I get to the door, I carefully peer through the peephole.

I'm met with a familiar grin. *Nate.* My heart jumps into my throat.

I throw the door open and immediately feel my brother's arms around me. "There she is! My little sister! An engaged woman!" Nate begins to whimper with faux tears. "She's growing up so fast…"

I suddenly realize Nate's not alone. I tear myself away from him and take in the sight. His wife Felicity is here with their two daughters. My mom and dad are tucked right behind them. Even Sasha is here. And, of course, the party wouldn't be complete without Wade and Emma. "Oh, my goodness! What are you doing here?" I squeal.

"Why don't you ask your *fiancé*?" Nate says with a waggle of his eyebrows.

I spin around and find Liam waiting in the hallway. "You did this?"

Liam cocks his head to the side bashfully.

God, I want to throw my arms around him and kiss him with all my might. I want to take him right into the bedroom and thank him properly. He knows me so well. The only thing that could have made this moment better was celebrating it with my family and friends. And here they all are.

"Come in, come in! Let's celebrate!" I announce excitedly, accepting all the hugs and love I possibly can from everyone.

Once everyone is inside and just Liam and I are in the hallway, I wrap my arms around him. "Thank you."

"You're welcome."

We kiss softly. "Later, I'll thank you properly," I whisper into his mouth.

"Don't get me any more riled up than I already am."

I throw my head back with laughter.

Champagne is uncorked, toasts are made, and the celebration begins. I don't leave Liam's side the entire time. I can't believe how far we've come. From hiding our love in the wildflowers of Indiana to being engaged and celebrating with my family... it's just like a dream.

A dream I never want to end.

About Alix Vaughn

Alix adores everything about billionaires: yachts, polo ponies, art collections, international travel and the immense power. Her characters usually come to her during a long soak in a hot lavender-scented bath, while sipping expensive tequila.

Reviews are very important for indie authors. Please consider leaving a review of Reunited With My Billionaire if you enjoyed the book. It doesn't have to be long, just a line or two. Thank you so much!

If you'd like to read a FREE book from Alix go to https://BookHip.com/N FXNJSC

Printed in Dunstable, United Kingdom